MY OLD SWEETHEART

My Old Sweetheart

Susanna Moore

Houghton Mifflin Company
Boston

10/1984
gen'l

Library of Congress Cataloging in Publication Data

Moore, Susanna.
My old sweetheart.

I. Title.
PS3563.0667M9   813'.54   82-6221
ISBN 0-395-32516-1   AACR2

Printed in the United States of America

V 10 9 8 7 6 5 4 3 2

for L.L.S.

MY OLD SWEETHEART

ONE

*T*HAT NIGHT the fields were on fire. The smell of the cane woke her: it was like sugar burning in the bottom of a pan. Three days before, she had Tōsi, the Japanese boy, move her cot to the sleeping porch. He thought it was because she loved the night-jasmine that covered that part of the house, the old part, but it was because she was waiting for the fires.

Usually Tōsi slept on a mat on the floor of her room. He did not sleep on the porch with her because the smell of the jasmine made his head hurt. He had nightmares: there were palm rats in the jasmine vines and he was afraid of them but he would never admit it. She agreed with him, that he should sleep in the hall, or wherever he liked. That way, when the fires began, there was no one to make her stay in bed. She stood at the screen all night watching the Filipinos burn the cane.

It was as light as day. It seemed impossible that everyone in the house could sleep through the caramel smell and the smoke, but she was glad. It made her watch more mysterious and holy. The tiny, dark silhouettes of the men moved like devils with pitchforks, black against the high flames. The sky was red. The smoke changed direction with the trade winds. The men worked all night, coaxing the fire. The dirt road kept the fires from jumping across to the bottom of the garden. Sometimes a spark escaped, like a comet, but it died quickly in the wet vines. She was never afraid. She was secretly and wickedly proud of her vigil and even this gave her pleasure.

It must have been near sunrise (it was always difficult to tell because the sky gave no sign that it was no longer night when the fields were on fire) when she thought she heard her mother scream. She ran quickly across the house to her room. No one else was awake in the Big House, perhaps because the roar of the fires distorted all sound.

Her mother was lying naked on her bed, on top of the covers. She must have dozed off. There was a long sear down her bare bony arm where the heating pad had fallen. Lily could not think why she would have felt the need of warmth in the thick heat of that night. Her father was not there. She wondered where he was.

There was a strange smell, not the smell of cane, or even of the wild crownflower her mother had let push its dense, waxy way into the room and down the walls so that the screens would no longer close. She was still asleep as Lily rolled her to the center of the bed. The smell came from her damp body. It was sweet and salty. Lily suddenly despised her for it. She ran back down the verandah to her room, even though by then she could hear her mother softly crying her name.

"Would you light my cigarette? I can't seem to do it with this funny burn."

They were sitting in the garden. The coop where Lily's

younger brother, Jack, kept his carrier pigeons was empty. He must have taken them to the Point again, Lily thought. The bamboo groves were smoky and clotted. The wind had fallen. The salmon haze from the fires had settled in the garden, paralyzing everything.

"You know I love you," her mother said. Lily inhaled from the cigarette before handing it to her. "Why must you always do that? You're fortunate your father isn't here."

"Where is he?" Lily asked. Anna shrugged and laid her big, heavy dark head back on the chair, closing her eyes. The cigarette hung lazily between her fingers. Lily wondered whether she would forget she held it until it burned down and scorched her fingers.

"Do you think you would like to do anything?" She did not lift her head or open her eyes.

Lily didn't answer.

"You burned yourself last night," she finally said.

"I know."

From across the garden they could hear Lily's sister, Jessie, playing in the dry plumeria leaves. Jessie was eight years old. There was quiet giggling. She must have been with her babysitter, a teen-age girl whom Lily thought very silly. The babysitter was only a few years older than Lily.

"Go tell them," her mother said. She did not lift her head. Lily waited, and her chair creaked.

"Go tell them. Those leaves are poisonous."

Lily went to tell them. "But come back," Anna called after her. "I have an idea."

⌫

Tōsi brought the jeep to the front and they climbed in over the open sides. Anna noticed when the jeep lurched several times and stalled that Tōsi was wearing a pair of big, black

3

lace-up shoes with no socks. Anna could see that the shoes were big enough so that he would not have had to untie the laces to slip them on.

Tōsi thought it was important to wear shoes when driving. He equated wearing shoes with being a man, although he himself was only twelve years old. He and Lily were the same age. They often had the same thoughts: Lily understood that he believed the shoes helped him to drive. But Anna did not know this. "Take off the shoes," she said.

"Why, Anna-san?"

"Because it is dangerous. If you do not, I will have to drive." Anna seldom used contractions. She spoke like someone who had learned English as a foreign language.

Tōsi removed the shoes unhappily and passed them over the seat to the children in the back, where Lily tried to find a large enough place to put them. Finally, she threw them over the side.

"Whose are they anyway?" she shouted, but they were moving at last, and he could not hear her.

It was the middle of summer. The black volcanic ridges and their deep, green valleys looked like the folds of an old velvet gown. Along the road, the sea was loud as it foamed white water against the lacy lava rock. The light and the moisture in the air made colors bright and true.

When they reached the end of the road, Tōsi parked jerkily under a casuarina tree. He said he would wait for them. He did not like the Cave. He would pick opihi instead. Anna and Jack and Lily were excited. They did not answer Tōsi, but jumped eagerly out of the jeep and went hurriedly through the sea grape.

When they reached the water, they had to scramble like monkeys over the wet rocks. There was a fishy smell of stale salt water. Lily saw Jack slip on the sharp, porous rock. He

4

stopped to study his foot carefully for signs of blood. Their mother was ahead of them. She did not look back, even when Jack called out. She is not the kind who bandages cuts, Lily thought. She is not like other mothers, who make grocery lists and wear undergarments. Other mothers do not forget that you go back to school in September, but other mothers, she thought, don't go into underground caves either. Although she preferred her mother, sometimes she was frightened.

Anna was already in the water. Using his rock scratches as an excuse, Jack yelled that he would wait with Tōsi. Lily waved and dived into the ocean.

She followed Anna's black head, round and shiny like a seal now that her hair was wet, bobbing through the green water, to the rocks at the base of the cliff. Anna's head went under. She did not come up. Big, round bubbles floated up slowly between Lily's legs and popped around her. She took extra air into her lungs and then she too disappeared beneath the surface.

Under water, pale green, it was suddenly silent as Lily followed a delicate trail of effervescence. She let some air rumble slowly out of her nose, saving the rest. The bubbles rose up past her open eyes. Her mother was gone. Lily slid herself along the spiky wall of rock, arms outstretched to keep from being thrown against it by the current. She found the cleft in the lava wall, felt for the opening in the rock, and quickly pulled herself inside.

At once she felt the temperature of the suddenly black water change. It grew colder and colder as she nervously kicked herself back up to the surface. She came up in darkness, spouting loudly, and breathed the cool, damp air. She was inside the Wet Cave. It was black all around her. There was not even a reflection on the water.

"Isn't it beautiful?" she heard her mother whisper. Her

5

voice echoed. Lily could not see her in the dark. They were inside the mountain in a high, vaulted cavern washed hollow for thousands of years by the sea. Hundreds of tiny pinholes in the lava dome arching above them let in constellations of light. It was like the clear night sky. There were too many sparks to be stars alone: lightning bugs, thought Lily.

"Where are you?" she asked.

She felt the inky water move around her and then a hand splashed behind her and she found her mother's arm.

"Are you afraid?"

Lily didn't answer. She was always a little afraid in the Cave, no matter how many times she had been there. She could just make out the shape of her mother's round head next to her. There was the sound of wings beating. She kept looking around to make sure that the small, green circle of light, the opening to the world, was still beneath them in the water.

"It is really like being on the very edge of the planet," Anna said exultantly.

Lily's legs began to tire from treading water. The water was cold. She began to lose her senses. It became impossible to judge distances — the distance from her to Anna and the distance from minute to minute. It made her dizzy. The pull of the tide rocked them gently, just enough to make the mock stars above them change position. There was a story about two boys who had been caught in the Cave when the neap tide was coming in. They were unable to find their way out through the green hole in the rising water. Lily wondered what it must have been like, feeling yourself move higher and higher into the night sky. Their dead bodies were marked with hundreds of little pricks where they had been crushed against the lava.

Lily said, "I am getting tired, Mother."

Anna spoke as though she had been startled. "Oh, my old sweetheart."

Lily heard her mother take in air, then the splash of her kick, then it was more silent than before. She floated on her back. She was alone in the Wet Cave. She turned over to watch the green light flicker off and on as Anna wiggled through the hole on her way back into the world, then she too dived down into it and smiled as she felt the stream of warm, living sea slide over her.

Anna used to order her clothes from magazines, a practice considered odd and vain by her wary neighbors, the wives of planters and retired colonialists, who never in their lives thought of ordering anything from Paris, let alone a black dress. These women bribed the local postman to keep them informed as to just what was in the long parcels covered with romantic and strange postage stamps that arrived seasonally at the Big House. And just when the planters' wives began to dress in solid colors, in imitation of Anna, she canceled her subscriptions to the magazines from Europe. They wearied of trying to keep up with her and eventually they stopped bribing the postman. It happened about the time of the territorial governor's ball.

For two days, the Big House had been deserted and silent. Even Tōsi, who rarely let Lily out of his sight, was missing. Lily roamed about, irritable and curious. The strange silence was replaced, a day before the ball, by mumbling and the shuffling of bare feet down straw-matted halls and the dragging of tapa-cloth sacks. In the kitchen, several of the young maids complained of headache and went to bed with bottles of pineapple wine. The children were neglected in the nursery as a strange, thick smell spread through the house. Lily sought solitude on the sleeping porch, but there was no refuge. Tōsi reappeared, exhausted and ill, and fell onto the verandah, where he slept heavily for half a day. In the sewing room, the old woman who ruled there weakly gave orders from her mat, surrounded by young girls with bruised and bleeding fingers. They were too tired to do anything but nod mutely and in unison when Lily demanded to know what was going on. She was furious. She went to the far side of the house to think. She must have fallen asleep. When she woke in the dark there was an overpowering smell and a swishing as servants crouched on their haunches.

At the end of a corridor, a tall, dark figure clouded in white was gliding toward her. The smell that had filled the house for days had now become unbearable. Her nostrils and eyes burned.

The white, wraithlike figure stopped before her. It was her mother. From the tips of her ears to her bare heels, she was sunk in a heavy, white cape. She smiled.

"I am leaving now," she said.

Lily just stared at her. She felt hatred for her mother and at the same time sudden, desperate sadness that, no matter how hard she might try, she would never be like her. Only Anna's big, dark head emerged from the white cape. There were no arms, no hands, no feet. Lily's head ached. She moved closer.

"I am afraid I cannot kiss you tonight," Anna said.

Tōsi ran up. He didn't even see Lily. He was too blinded by Anna. Lily took a step nearer. Only then did she understand that Anna was covered, thicker than any jungle patch, in hundreds and hundreds of white gardenias.

"Do you think, at last, they will like me?" She laughed quietly and turned and glided back down the hall. Tōsi was kneeling. Lily kicked him and ran away, weeping.

<hr/>

Although it was always Tōsi's job to wake the children each morning at six-thirty, the next morning he did not come until well past seven. He said it was because the kitchen was in an uproar. Lily's father refused to eat his usual breakfast of two guavas and black jasmine tea. Someone had left a newspaper on the table open to the society page. A columnist called Pupule Plumeria described Anna, who "stalked traditionally late into the ballroom and to the gasps of the shocked island crème de la crème dropped her full-length cape, made entirely of four thousand fresh white gardenias, onto the floor . . ."

Never before in the history of the Big House had Doctor Sheridan walked away from his breakfast. Tōsi brought Lily the guavas as a special treat and she ate them greedily, even the skins, while Tōsi watched. She felt as if she were destroying evidence. Tōsi held out his hand patiently for the stems, but she shook her head and threw them over the side of the verandah. He watched her silently, with great seriousness, as he always did.

Their first memory was of each other. Tōsi remembered that once, long ago, something had fallen heavily on him from above. When he picked himself up he discovered it was Lily, who had leaped on him from a monkey-pod tree. Lily recalled it differently. Tōsi ordered her down from the tree. She did not want to come down. He insisted. She jumped on top of him with all her spring and might. They must have been about three years old and, although they had been together since Lily's first breath, their life together, as far as they knew, began with Lily's knocking him to the ground. It was an apt beginning. Neither of them would have admitted it, perhaps neither of them knew it, consciously, but Tōsi's job was to catch Lily, just as Lily's job was to jump.

They did not compete with each other, as might have been expected of two children who were always together, nor were they particularly curious about each other, although they were of different sex and color and temperament. They were similar physically, except for race: thin and wiry, with thick black hair cut blunt, and round, dark eyes in serious, smooth faces.

Together, they made a perfect child. Apart and imperfect, they became vague and indecisive and withdrawn. Later, when they finally were separated and Lily was sent to the school in town, she suffered very much. He did, too, although he at least was allowed to stay home with Anna.

Her grief worsened when her father sent Tōsi to Japan. For a long time, perhaps always, Lily believed it was because of her that Tōsi was sent away for three months every year. It happened when they were eight, when her father came into the playroom one afternoon and overheard Lily doing an imitation of the Japanese gardener, pretending to be a samurai, decapitating orchids. She was very funny. For some reason, they had climbed into Jessie's playpen, and Tōsi was lying on his back, staring up adoringly at Lily, who was shouting "Banzai!" and "Ha-So!" Tōsi was laughing so hard that he held himself so that he wouldn't wet his pants, and Lily was so carried away with her success that she didn't stop when she saw her father, but exaggerated her play-acting. Later, she blamed herself for showing off. One week later, when Tōsi was sent to Japan to study, she knew it was because of her samurai show.

It was never again the same for them. When he returned that first time, he was self-aware and secretive. He held something inside of him, out of Lily's reach and understanding. He knew what it was, but he would not have been able to explain what had altered him and altered them. Lily grieved.

Tōsi was no longer her twin. He was changed — and Lily was shocked. He was shy and grateful. He began to wait on her, to clean up after her, and to follow Anna around, looking for things he could do for her. He acted as if he were in Lily's debt. It infuriated and hurt her. She went to her mother. Anna could not, or would not, explain it either, except to say that Sheridan wanted Tōsi to have a sense of his own country and culture. It did not make sense to Lily. Perhaps you were too much together, her mother said gently. Lily decided at that moment that she would never belong to any country.

She was very lonely. Tōsi busied himself on the plantation, helping out. He began studying Japanese with Sheridan. He even began to sleep in a different part of the house. It was a mystery Lily could not solve. She was heartbroken. Anna spoke to Sheridan, and Lily was invited to share in the special lessons each afternoon, but only after Tōsi had completed his private, more serious, tutoring with Sheridan.

It was especially confusing to Lily because she seemed to be the only one who thought Tōsi was changed. Her mother was busy with her own lessons, all meant to make her more intellectually alert or more physically active; Jack and Jessie were little and unaware; and Tōsi, Tōsi was busy learning how to tie an obi and make green tea for Anna when she came home all shriveled and shivering from her scuba lesson.

It took Lily a long time to recover. When she finally did, she too had changed. She was not shy and humble. She was more isolated. She did not love Tōsi any less. She gave in to his mysterious gratitude. She let him take care of her and she convinced herself, and even grew to believe, that people knew what they were doing, that their actions were deliberate and thought-out and purposeful. She especially tried to believe that: that people were full of purpose. She might not be able to understand why they acted the way they did, but surely *they* must know. Otherwise, it would not make any sense at all.

TWO

J DREAMED of Anna again last night. It was the same as
always. I search everywhere for something I have mis-
placed and must find again. It is a matter of life or death.
When I wake fully, covered in perspiration, I find myself out
of bed, hovered over a desk pulling things out of drawers, or
sitting on the edge of the bed holding an overturned wastebasket.

I have wakened like this in so many strange rooms in so
many strange countries. Last night I even dreamed that the
girl Christmas was my sister. And Anna took care of her.

At breakfast there was a letter from my sister, Jessie. I
didn't open it, although I was alone. Isn't it funny that as a
grown woman I still prefer guavas for breakfast? Everything
reminds me of Anna. I suppose it is very difficult to forgive a
woman covered, and covered with great deliberation, in
thousands of white flowers. And yet, every part of me aches
for it. I wonder whether my father ever aches for it. Would we
have preferred the ordinary? It has forced me to go to ironic

and ludicrous attempts to appear ordinary to my own child. But even here, where the black, island servants swear to me that they are out of season, I am stifled and thrilled by the constant odor of invisible gardenias.

I have not seen my sister Jessie for some time. Or my brother. It is difficult for us to be together. Once we left the island, each in a different direction, we stayed away and apart. I left when I was sixteen. Jack disappeared when he was seventeen. Jessie made it only to fifteen. It seems strange now that Father let us all go so easily. (I told him that I wanted to travel and the next day there was an airplane ticket on the table outside my room. It was made out in my name, but there was no destination. For years I felt the shame of his disappointment when I chose to go to my grandmother in North Philadelphia instead of the Borobudar Temple in central Java.)

Today I took Jessie's letter with me to the club bar overlooking the ocean. Far below on the beach, my daughter, little Anna, and Tōsi were walking back and forth, trying to make friends with other children. They did not seem to be having much luck.

The letter was very short and, like my sister, to the point. I read it cautiously:

Dear Lil,

I am very sorry not to have written sooner but as usual I didn't have your new hotel and, as you are quite aware, you seem to leave behind wakes of injured suitors whom I just couldn't ask.

I have rather strange news. Father has disappeared (at last). When I did not receive the old six-monthly trust payment, I tried to reach him and apparently he has been gone for some time. No one thought it weird, even though he sold the Big House and most of the land. You, I know, will be especially thrilled to learn that the Eucalyptus Maze was bought by a haole developer who plans to build an ice-skating rink! The first ever in Hawaii.

I love you and miss you. Will you ever be coming this way? There are houses to rent here, you know. Give little Anna a big kiss — does she remember me? Love to Tōs.

Jessie

Also enclosed was a gift subscription to a new California magazine called *One-Parent Families*. She had given the Big House as my address, although I had not lived there for ten years.

I walked to the beach, down the stone steps cut from the cliff. Little Anna seemed to have found company. She was sitting cross-legged in the sand with another little girl and her mother. As always, she greeted me with fervor, as though she had not seen me in months.

Tōsi pulled over a beach chair and I sat down.

"Hello," said the woman. "What a sweet little girl you have." She was looking at me oddly.

"Yes," I said. It would be foolish to think that Tōsi, little Anna and I did not make a strange family. Usually we stayed in places where they left us alone. "What's your little girl's name?" I asked politely.

"John."

"Oh, I'm sorry. Anna, have you been playing with John?" Anna looked at me and made a face.

"Are you American?" asked the woman.

"Yes. I suppose I am."

"Oh," she said, deciding not to be insulted. "But you have an accent. I was trying to place you."

"Yes. People often say that. I don't know why."

"Your friend has an accent too."

"My friend does," I said. My friend Tōsi was staring out to sea. Anna put her thumb in her mouth, watching me.

"What does your husband do?" the woman asked.

"I don't have a husband."

"You've been staying up on the bluff quite a while now. I've seen you."

The woman dusted off the skirt of her bathing suit.

"Come, Anna, shall we have a walk?" I asked.

Anna shook her head and leaped into my lap. The other child stealthily grabbed her pail and shovel.

"She really *is* lovely," the woman said. Her tone was very wistful. She even sounded sorry.

"I'm going for a walk," I said. I lifted Anna screaming from my lap.

When I reached the top of the cliff, I looked back. The little group below was exactly as I had left them, only now they were motionless, staring up at me. Or so it seemed, for I had forgotten my glasses and the letter in the bar.

I sat down and opened Jessie's letter again. When we came to this island in the Caribbean last week it was enough like the island where I was born that I became alarmed and confused the moment I saw from the window of the airplane the dark gray sea changing to green, and the white water breaking over the reef.

During the long drive to the hotel, I wildly identified every flower, plant and bird I could spot from the taxi. No one else in the car spoke. Even little Anna was silent. Later I tried to explain to Tōsi that suddenly being on an island so like home was like finding myself in an old, recurring dream I hoped I had forgotten. But he needed no explanation because he is benignly convinced that I am given to excess wherever I find myself.

"You were happy," he said the next morning.

"I wasn't. I was excited. I was upset."

"You like to be upset. It's an island."

"No Zen, thank you."

He walked out, smiling, letting the thin, screened door swing so that it bounced back and forth. Ten minutes later, a black boy in a golf cart drove onto the grass. He carried a case of cold champagne into the kitchen.

"From the gentleman in the dress," he said expressionlessly. They are not accustomed to kimonos in the West Indies.

THREE

LILY had some notion that when her mother's green convertible was parked, the word "Chevrolet" on each tire cap had to be horizontal. Her mother believed her and spent half an hour one hot afternoon trying to park so that the word was straight and legible on each wheel. Lily crouched at the curb, instructing her back and forth while they waited for Anna's best friend, Tigger, to come out of the local beauty shop, a house at the end of the road where an ex-Hollywood make-up artist had set up a hair dryer and a sink with a hose in her front parlor. Tigger said the woman had made up Myrna Loy.

Tigger was very tall, with red hair and blue eyes. She came from Texas. She was like those women who play the second lead in movies, foils for the heroines, sarcastic and droll and looking for rich husbands because they are, as they are always telling you, very wise in the ways of the world. Anna thought she was funny and straightforward and that those were qualities of some worth. Tigger wanted to be like Anna but pretended to disapprove of her. Tigger accused her of being naïve and soft-hearted. Nevertheless, she always borrowed Anna's furs when she went to the Mainland for, as she put it, "the thee-ater."

She finally appeared, her hair redder than usual. She stared at Anna and Lily from across the street, then walked to the driver's side of the car, shaking her head.

"I'm sure you have a good explanation, sugar, unless it's the rum again."

"We're trying to get the Chevrolets straight," Anna said. She smiled pleasantly.

"The what?"

Anna pointed to the tires. Lily came around the side of the car just in time to see Tigger throw all her American fashion magazines onto the front seat.

"Get in," Tigger said wearily to Lily, shaking her new red head.

They were on their way to the airport. Anna liked driving to the airport and it was not often that she could get Tigger, or anyone for that matter, to make the long, hot excursion with her. She always stopped just outside the corrugated-tin hut that served as the terminal to buy flowers from the old lei sellers in their grass shacks. She always bought forty dollars' worth, enough leis for a hundred people, and laid them gently on wet ti leaves Tōsi had already prepared on the back seat.

Tigger indulged all this, but with some boredom. "Who're we meeting today, sugar?"

"No one."

"Could've fooled me," said Tigger. She yawned exaggeratedly and cleaned her big sunglasses slowly and put them on.

Tigger knew there would be no planes arriving. Anna and Lily knew too. There were only six planes a week, and they came in at night.

"I like to come here. Someday I am going to get on one," Anna said.

Tigger laughed harshly. "One what?" she asked.

"One airplane," Anna said patiently. Lily always got a sick feeling in her stomach when her mother said things like that: someday I'm going to get on one.

Anna walked inside, leaving the flower leis behind.

"You know, you could always wear a grass skirt and give those flower things away. Kiss a tourist and get your picture in the paper," Tigger said. Anna laughed.

"Her picture's in the paper enough," Lily said.

"You sound just like your father," Anna said happily over her shoulder.

They walked through the terminal hut. The porters and clerks nodded and smiled at Anna. She knew most of them by name now. The hut had a dirt floor. At one end a small brown man sat sleepily at a wooden desk with a microphone to announce the infrequent arrivals and departures.

Out on the field, Anna leaned up against the rickety fence that kept visitors from falling under the wheels of the big, heavy, propeller planes. It was windy and Tigger looked at her watch.

"What time is it?"

"I have no idea," Anna said.

They stood quietly because it was impossible to talk over the sound of the plane taking off. A few people waved as the plane taxied down the ground-coral runway. One old man, barefoot, sang a chant. The plane lifted heavily and slowly.

"Thank God," said Tigger.

"It reminds me of my mother. You know, my father owned all of the railroads in Pennsylvania," Anna said.

Tigger removed her sunglasses and stared at her.

"So they say," Anna murmured, looking away.

Together, they turned from the fence and walked back to the car. Anna drove home along the sea, a longer way but one that she knew Lily preferred. Lily sat in the back, balanced on the edge of the flower-laden seat, her arms around Anna's bare shoulders.

"Lily and I went out at dusk looking for marlin," Anna said. "Sighted two, hooked one. Earl thinks I have learned awfully fast."

"You can't even eat the goddamn things," Tigger said. "*I*, for one, went to see that play *Macbeth* at the college. They had the cutest actors. I wish you'd come. Better than circling for hours in the heat looking for a goddamn fish."

"Did you like it?" Anna asked politely.

"Well, to tell you the truth, sugar, I found it a little confusing, even with the program. There's this terrible battle in the beginning, you see, and then Thane Macbeth and his friend, I can't remember his name . . ."

"Banquo?" Anna asked hesitantly.

"You told me you hadn't seen it!" Tigger said indignantly.

Anna laughed. "I haven't!"

"You bitch! How did you know his name?"

"Didn't you read it in school?" Anna was trying hard not to laugh. Tigger stared sullenly at the horizon. "What *did* you do in school?" Anna asked, laughing again. Tigger tried not to smile. She did not often have a chance to make Anna feel sorry.

Lily did not understand why Anna was laughing or why Tigger was so angry. She was confused. The leis on the seat had lost their moisture, and the ivory-colored tuberose were beginning to turn brown. She held her arms over them protectively as the wind from the channel blew over them. When they got home, she and Tōsi would hand the leis around to their favorites. All the time she thought about the flowers she was listening to Anna and Tigger.

"Lily," Anna said, twisting around in her seat, "did you know that your Aunt Tigger got her name when she was a girl because she could not pronounce the word 'trigger'?" Anna began to laugh again and Tigger tried not to, but could not keep herself from yelping loudly in delight. Even Lily smiled, her long, stalky arms held over the wilting flowers.

⟨᠆᠊᠊⟩

Lily's brother Jack, who was nine years old, kept a coop of twenty carrier pigeons. Surprisingly, no one else cared much about them, although Lily once caught one of the gardeners stealing the eggs to eat. She did not tell Jack because she felt he might kill the man.

Every Thursday, Jack gently laid six of his birds in an old blue baby blanket in the wicker basket mounted on the handlebars of his bike and rode three miles down the dusty road to the Point. Every Thursday for the last two years he opened the blanket and with trembling, cupped hands gracefully threw each bird into the air. Then he got back on his bike and pedaled as fast as he could the three miles uphill to the house, in the wild and irrational hope that someday he would be there to greet his pigeons. Once they used to line up on the hill — children, housemaids, fishermen, his mother — to watch the race between birds and boy, although they all knew, after the first few outings, that he could never possibly arrive home before the birds.

By the time he climbed the hill, tanned legs pumping and cramped, the heat-dazed birds had long since tucked their heads under their wings and gone to sleep for the day. But he never gave up hope and never even noticed when the spectators quite soon disappeared from their stations on the hill.

Sometimes, though, Lily waited for him. He was thrilled to see her. It was unusual for Lily to be alone. She was always with Tōsi, and they were always with Anna, so he was surprised as well as pleased to see her, sitting in the tall grass at the top of the hill, her chin resting on her knees, squinting into the sun.

When he got to the top of the hill, she rose up straight from her nest in the grass.

"Are they back?" he asked anxiously.

She considered whether or not to lie. "About fifteen minutes ago," she said finally and realized that she had made the right decision. Jack did not mind that the pigeons beat him home every time. Everyone else minded.

"Do you want to go swimming with me?"

"Where's Tōsi?" He wheeled his bike under a banyan and pulled down the rusty kick stand with his toes.

"Having his lesson. I have forty-five minutes before mine begins."

They went to make sure the coop was properly fastened. "Look what I found," Jack said and he pulled out from under a layer of newspaper a small black and white photograph of a man in an army uniform. The man was smiling shyly, standing in front of what looked like a demolished bridge. For a moment, it reminded Lily of someone she knew. The man in the photograph had white hair and white eyebrows, although he looked very young. "Don't tell anyone," Jack said, "but it's Father." Lily took the picture from him and studied it closely. "It can't be," she said. He took it from her and carefully slid it back under the newspaper.

As they hurried across the lawn to the water they could hear their father's voice through the shuttered doors of his library saying, "The city, with an unusually high Buddhist population, convinced itself that this was the reason it had remained untouched throughout the war . . . In truth — "

The voice stopped; then Tōsi's voice could just be heard. Lily listened. She looked awkward, standing stiff on the big lawn as though her stillness would bring Tōsi's voice nearer. Jack was envious of Tōsi. He liked it when Tōsi was having his lesson. He liked it when Tōsi went to Japan. He missed him when he was away, but he also was happy to see him go because it meant that he had more of Lily's time. He loved her. She was full of strength, it seemed to him. She knew what to do. He could count on her. He could not count on his mother. He worshiped his mother, he would die for her and she for him, but he could not depend on her. The time the manager's dogs turned over the coop and began biting off pigeons' heads, it was Lily who had streaked across the lawn, throwing at the crazed dogs sharp twigs and leaves she stripped from tree branches as she ran along. Her hands bled, but his mother took one look at a quivering, headless pigeon and fainted.

It was because he worshiped his mother and could not count on her that he began raising pigeons in the first place. Without knowing why, he felt the need to care for something, to hold it alive and warm in his small hands, to protect it. This small thing in his small hands that needed protecting was, of course, himself. Since he had never come to feel safe in Anna's willing but hopeless hands, he made himself the steadfast, reliable keeper. He devoted himself to twenty ring-eyed birds he had hatched from eggs. He did everything but sit on them himself.

Sheridan had helped him. He took Jack early one evening to buy pigeon eggs at the Filipino farm where the man bred cocks for fighting. The farmer wanted them to stay for the fight, offering them front-row places in the dirt, but Sheridan had refused and after many bows and handshakes they had walked home in the dark, his father smoking and looking at the millions of stars, Jack carrying the warm eggs in a soiled brown paper bag, trying not to jump at the sound of lizards rustling energetically in the vines. They stopped to watch the fishermen prepare the gasoline-rag torches for fishing at night. The strong smell as the men doused the rags made Jack feel sick, but he did not let Sheridan know, and when they went on, he felt better.

Jack wanted his father to admire him. He did not think about love — that was reserved for Anna — but he did want Sheridan's respect. Even if it had not been for Anna, Sheridan did not require or give great emotions. He was a detached and elegant observer. When they were still very small, the children had been allowed in Sheridan's rooms, where they were encouraged to look at, and even touch, his extraordinary collection of Buddhas and books and textiles and carvings. They had learned early on that their father was a discerner, a person who knew what was fine and cared about what was fine. Jack could not remember ever having wrestled with his father (the very idea would have been alarming to Jack), but he could remember a time when his father praised him for some shells he brought home from the Point, black shells that Jack had thought ordinary and dull, but shells that Sheridan admired for that same black dullness. Jack realized then that there was never any anticipating his father's pleasure, any knowing exactly what he would approve or dismiss, and that it would be best for him, Jack, to keep quiet and wait to hear what Sheridan thought. Sheridan's observations were original and witty, and Jack learned, without even realizing he was being taught, many things. Jack did not think his father did not care about him. The very fact that Sheridan would take the time to help Jack select the most "interestingly" speckled pigeon eggs was proof enough of affection, and in some additionally mysterious way Jack understood that what he learned from his father, what they all learned from him, about gradations of age and hue and light and shade, were subtleties that applied also to other things, grander and more difficult things, like sorrow and hate and love.

❧

Sheridan and Anna took their three children to nine o'clock Mass every Sunday. Anna had been born a Catholic. She wore her religion like a flattering hat. She felt it enhanced her, brought out her best features and made her taller. Her uncle was a bishop in Africa, and she often bragged that he had once promised to give her the big ruby-encrusted crucifix he wore around his neck if she would kiss him on the mouth. She had not seen any impropriety in this (nor in later telling the story many times) and she was quite shocked when, after she had kissed him, at his insistence not the one time but three times, he refused to give her the crucifix.

Sheridan did not particularly like this story. He was a late convert from the Episcopal Church, that "high-falukey" religion, Anna called it. She saw his conversion as a political as well as a moral victory, a crossing over to the correct side, like a Republican becoming a Democrat. She had told Lily that this miracle was the child's doing: once when Lily was very small she had asked him how his morning in church had been, and he, who had not been to a church in years, had lied. He said afterward (according to Anna) that he would "never lie to that innocent child again" and went straight to the monsignor for religious instruction. Lily secretly did not believe this story for one minute. It did not sound at all like her father. It sounded like something her mother would make up.

Their appearance at church each Sunday morning was important to Anna. She dressed in a completely unsuitable way in tight white gloves and pale silk stockings. She wore a heavy lace mantilla three feet wide. She made Lily wear shoes. The other women wore loose-fitting muu-muus and pinned flowers in their hair, and the men did not bother to tuck their light cotton shirts into their baggy trousers. Anna liked it when Sheridan wore a cream linen suit.

It all made Lily irritable. That it was a success for Anna, that the island people admired her and even looked forward to seeing her new outfit each Sunday, made Lily even more annoyed. Perhaps it was the hunger as well as the attention that made her so upset. They fasted from midnight the night before in order to be pure for communion. Lily often thought she might faint, with the sweating and the staring.

The pastor, Father Melchior, was a Belgian missionary. No one could understand a word he said, not even in Latin when they tried to follow the litany in their missals. The parishioners did not like their priest. Sheridan's position was enhanced.

In many ways, he was the most important man there each Sunday. Everyone stopped to talk to him, to shake his hand, to ask him to feel a goiter or to look into a grandfather's rheumy eyes. Even Father Melchior, waiting at the heavy wooden doors as his flock stumbled out into the blinding morning sunlight, seemed overjoyed to see Sheridan. The priest had problems with his stomach, from eating flower bulbs during the War he said, and sometimes he would take

Sheridan's long, elegant hand and put it on top of his belly and cover it with his own two hands.

Lily and Jack and Jessie, pale with nausea, would linger uncomfortably in the harsh light and pant like puppies while Sheridan gracefully disengaged himself from the priest and Anna blushed and flirted. It was hard for the children not to break into a run for the car when they were finally released.

There was always a new, clean but grease-stained, white cardboard box in the back of the car, full of sweet bread and Portuguese malasadas. It was Lily's job to open the warm box and as the car started off, the wind cooling them now as they pulled off shoes and wet socks with sugar-coated fingers, Anna reached behind without looking and Lily put some buttered bread in her gloved hand. They were all quiet, concentrating on eating.

Sheridan stopped the car in front of the Big House gates and Tōsi stepped from behind the gatepost and jumped into the back next to Lily. He did not have to go to Mass. To Lily's confusion, her father did not want Tōsi to be a Catholic. She thought it particularly unfair because she sensed that he did not especially want her to be Catholic either, but had given her as a sacrifice to Anna's convention. Sheridan, with his usual politeness, was simply behaving as he always did: going to Mass for him was no different from any other domestic nicety that pleased Anna, a gesture like offering her a chair or taking her in to dinner. He expected Lily to be polite too.

On the beach road, they drove parallel to the white coral sea wall. Sheridan smoked as he steered with one hand and inclined his head slightly at the driver of each infrequently passing car. He must have heard the children and Anna talking and laughing but his smiling face gave no sign. He was thinking about other things. Jessie counted and re-counted the remaining rolls, calculating how many had gone to each person. She knew her father never ate one, so she did not include him. It was Jessie's self-assumed job to keep track of everything around her. As was inevitable, it being a prerequisite of the personality, she always felt short-changed. Perhaps it was because she was the youngest. It never occurred to Lily or Tōsi or Jack to worry about how much they were getting and consequently they always got enough.

"This last one's mine," Jessie announced. She did not look like the other two children (that is, she did not look like her mother. "She's not Irish," Anna would say, sadly studying Jessie's pale face and light, pale eyes).

Sheridan turned down the bumpy lane to the water. He stopped where the rock turned to sand and they all got out and undressed in the shade, the girls removing their thin, soaked sundresses, the men their shirts and trousers. They all wore their bathing suits underneath.

Except for Anna, they busied themselves adjusting straps on rubber masks and big, green fins, spitting into masks, rubbing the warm saliva on the glass, twisting mouthpieces on snorkels. It took a long time. It was especially difficult for Jessie, who was finicky, to get her straps adjusted to her liking, and while Tōsi helped her, Anna wandered back and forth patiently, picking empty beer bottles and dirty picnic plates out of the sea grape and burying them in a shallow hole in the sand she dug with her toes. Anna never used a mask or snorkel. She said it was interesting enough on this planet. Lily liked to watch her mother's body curving languidly on the surface while she, Lily, pretended to be chasing yellow tigerfish. No one ever noticed that Lily swam with her mask facing upward into the light, watching Anna's long, weightless body, because they were all looking downward, busily spotting brain coral and moray eels.

They were swimming to tiny Chinaman's Hat, a green

29

islet shaped exactly like a coolie's straw hat. It was only fifty yards offshore. The side facing the beach was sheer and rocky and inaccessible, rising straight to its little pointed crown, but the ocean side held a miniature, protected bay with a tiny and powdery pink-sand beach.

Finally in the water, Anna was first to round the head and she joyfully yelled back that the beach was deserted, forgetting that they couldn't hear her with their heads under water. She could hear them, though, their grunts coming through the periscope-tops of their snorkels as they tried to get each other's attention. Now and then it even seemed that one of them laughed raucously underwater.

Anna pulled herself up on the warm beach and felt the quick thrill of being alone — unheard and unseen. The feeling was made finer because she knew it would last only until the others splashed noisily ashore. She took off her bathing suit. She looked like a girl, her body clean and lean as a bleached bone. For that moment, the world and her body in it felt free of excess. She felt sexless.

She was day-dreaming that she would make a good castaway, imagining how she would fashion a drinking cup from a hollow coconut shell, a fishing line from dried sea-weed, when she heard a giggle come from behind some big rocks at the end of the beach. She felt embarrassed and she smiled a shy, apologetic smile at the rocks. There was another giggle.

She looked out to sea, where her husband and her children were diving and surfacing excitedly like playful whales blowing air out their spouts. They must have found something. Lily seemed to be headed for the beach, although she could not be sure whose small brown head was coming closer.

She put on her suit. She considered for a moment that she

had imagined the sound, that some ancient spirit of the place was laughing at her. She went to the rocks and peered over the top. Squatting low on their heels were two teen-age girls. She remembered something Sheridan had once said about Orientals being best able to squat like that because their leg tendons were short. Had he said that? She wondered. One of the girls looked familiar. Anna particularly noticed that this girl, the one she thought she knew, wore an old, black nylon swimsuit with gathers on the sides. Anna knew it was old because the color had turned to an almost iridescent dark green from too much salt and sun, and some of the gathers had lost their elastic around the girl's full breasts. The girl looked like a mixture: white and something else. The other girl stared boldly at Anna. Anna looked around quickly and saw Lily standing chest-high in the foaming white water, sliding her mask back on her head. Lily waved at her.

The girl she did not know laughed loudly at Anna and then mockingly covered her mouth. The girl in the black suit just stared at Anna and smiled, not with meanness but with curiosity and friendliness. Anna remembered then that this was the girl Christmas. She was called that because she had been born on Christmas Day.

Lily was coming out of the water, hopping awkwardly from one foot to the other as she removed her fins.

Anna ran down to the water. "Don't come out!" she shouted above the sound of the surf. She waved her arms. She had not had time to tie the straps of her suit and her top slipped down.

"What is it, Mother?" Lily was smiling and squinting.

"There are jellyfish all over the beach," Anna said, backing Lily into deeper water. "All over," she said, looking back over her shoulder.

"That's funny," Lily said, jumping and trying to see over her mother's head. The beach was empty.

"Isn't it funny," Anna said. She lowered herself into the water. Lily looked at her carefully.

"There aren't any in the water," she said.

"I know. Isn't it strange," Anna said, swimming at her to keep her from going closer to the beach. "Come on, let's tell them," Anna said. Her body floated over a small wave.

"But they'll want to rest," Lily said. Anna was already halfway to the others, waving Lily after her. Lily looked back at the deserted beach as she put her fins back on. It was peaceful and still. She could not see any jellyfish. She could see her mother's footprints, half-erased now by the tide. There was the cry of a sea bird. She heard Jessie groan as Anna reached them with the bad news.

⸺

The whole way back to the plantation, Anna was silent. Lily sat directly behind her in the car. She too was silent. The other children busily examined and discussed the sea specimens they had collected. Lily thought her mother had behaved oddly on Chinaman's Hat. She was used to her mother behaving oddly, so she attached no great moral weight to this observation. She simply wondered what had upset her.

Lily felt that she understood her mother. Anna had few secrets from her. This intimacy was, perhaps, Anna's way of shifting responsibility from herself to Lily, for it was certainly Lily who resided in the real world, alert and watchful, while Anna passed her long days on an island all her own. It was Lily who served as the swinging bridge that joined Anna to the mainland, for Lily was flexible and useful.

Her entire life was Anna. All Lily wanted was to make things right for her. She was tireless. Just how it had become her concern, rather than her mother's, was not a question to trouble her. She did not begrudge one moment of service. That this might be dangerous, to Lily, to Anna, to all of them, was a notion too sophisticated for Lily and too sensible for Anna. If anyone could have saved them it would have been Sheridan, but he had long since allowed himself the luxury of objectivity. He was affectionate and fair-minded, but these were not qualities particularly adequate to rescue a woman in enormous trouble and the child she had taken along as her companion.

Lily knew that her mother was in trouble. It was one of the reasons she felt no resentment in her job. She knew that she told lies, that she took too many pills, that she believed herself to be ignorant and helpless and that she was bound to Sheridan with a fierce passion.

That she should be in the position of wanting so ardently to make things right for her mother was, of course, that same mother's doing. Anna had so drawn Lily into her maternity, into her femaleness and her magic, that Lily could not be faulted for wanting to fix everything, even if she didn't understand what it was that needed fixing.

Anna was not too clear about what she wanted fixed, either. She may not even have known what was wrong. What she did know, and brood about, and hoped would be right forever, was her husband's sexual desire for her. She was unsure about her instincts, her intelligence and what she would have called her "goodness," but she was sure about her ability to arouse her husband. Because it was the only thing in which she had any confidence, she held on to it and made it more important than was necessary. It was true, he did desire her, especially in the beginning, but he grew to be embarrassed and, eventually, contemptuous of her efforts to keep him interested. His delicacy, his discernment, were repelled by her. She exercised, she was fastidious about her person, she flirted with other men just to make him jealous, she oiled and creamed her pretty body, she read the more serious women's magazines and vowed never to greet him with bad news, she waited up for him long into the night, rubbing scent behind her ears — and all this was too obvious and dumb for him. It was not subtle. Sheridan, in his awful snobbery, was upset by deliberation. He wanted everything to be unstudied, ingenuous and without effort. He was all wrong about her, of course. Anna was nothing if not natural. You could not be more unschooled than Anna was in the beginning. She would have been the first to admit it, in an honest moment. That is why she took all those exhausting courses and programs. She studied everything she thought might please him. She worked very hard. Without his ever knowing it, because he was already too absorbed in his own constant study and because it would never have occurred to him to consult her, she had become an eager and gifted student. What was worse, she never even knew it herself. (She was able, in a short time and without the least trace of pride or self-awareness, to spot a rare eighteenth-century Haritsu lacquer box in a curio shop and bring it home, only to slip it into her lingerie drawer for fear that she had bought a piece of junk.) She never learned to trust herself.

How could Lily help her? For all her enthusiasm, Anna could not help herself. She could not make out her place. When she first arrived on the island, a bride, with her new sables and crocodile shoes and Dior suits, she had immediately realized her mistake. She knew, too, that it was not just a question of fashion. It was thoughtless of Sheridan to let her buy things he knew she would never use. Perhaps he was afraid to tell her right away that the life he had envisioned for them did not require velvet cocktail hats with little veils. It did not, in fact, require shoes.

So she was emotionally unprepared, in addition to having nothing appropriate to wear. He was very generous with her and she was able to go out right away and be fitted for day muu-muus and party muu-muus, but it left her confused and ill at ease. She felt that he had tricked her in some way. She put away her finery. (Lily once found a fur muff stuffed into the vegetable drawer of a refrigerator. She thought it was a preserved animal.) She tried to accommodate herself to island ways. It was very difficult. Society, made up of kamaaina families descended from the nineteenth-century sea captains and missionaries who settled the island, was closed to newcomers like Anna and Sheridan, no matter how charming or rich or well-born they might be. It did not bother Sheridan. The idea of belonging was not one that would have ever occurred to him. But Anna was like a stranded mermaid.

She did not entirely give up the fantasy of how she wanted to live. She talked about sending Lily to boarding school in Virginia and Jack to Massachusetts (it might as well have been the moon to the children) and she sent away for things like the *Dames of Colonial America Cook Book* and handmade log carriers from Maine and smoked Virginia hams. It was a very hot climate in which to be eating big roast hams before a blazing wood fire.

Sheridan tried to help her. He spent hours with her on the fishing boat (she was very sick) and taught her to eat raw fish with chopsticks and to drive a jeep and to cut a pineapple and even to paddle an outrigger canoe.

There were some things she did quite naturally. She was someone who had watched her exhausted mother wash other people's laundry until three o'clock in the morning and she was, in her turn, very kind and natural with her own servants. There was nothing they would not do for her. And there was much that they did do. They felt protective of her. They kept many things from Sheridan.

Once, she saw an advertisement in the paper of a house for sale. There was a photograph. It was a new house, built in one of those cheap, overnight developments that Sheridan deplored, an ugly series of empty lots and bare streets cut from the jungle. But the house was in the "New England style," with shutters and a false attic window and a chimney and even a white picket fence. It was grotesque, set against banana and mango trees, but Anna thought it was beautiful. She made an appointment with the real estate salesman and somehow she got Sheridan to go with her to see it. She still wore high heels during the day then and the expedition began very badly when her heels sank into the mud of the as yet unseeded front lawn and Sheridan had to pull her out. She had to take off the shoes to get to the house and by the time she reached the front door (dark green, like the shutters, with a big brass knocker) and the frowning real estate agent, her feet were so soiled, he would not let her inside his model home. Sheridan was furious — not at Anna; she had behaved with her customary single-minded naïveté — but at the man, who told them they'd have to make another appointment. Why Sheridan even allowed himself to be talked into look-ing at the house is a mystery. He certainly had no intention of leaving the plantation. Perhaps it was mistaken indulgence. He was still in love with her then. He helped her down the unfinished driveway, her pretty, well-tended feet pricked and pierced by the sharp pebbles, her stockings shot with a new tear every few steps. By the time they got to the car, her stockings were in shreds. He saw that she was humiliated and put his hand on top of hers, folded primly in her lap, as they drove past the NEW ENGLAND ISLAND ALOHA ESTATES sign and back into the jungle.

"You must toughen up those feet," he said. "Three hours every day without shoes working up to walking across hot lava in two months." He kept looking over at her as he drove. She looked straight ahead. The convertible top was down, and the shadows of the overhanging trees cast them in and out of darkness.

"Then we'll have the poi-eating lessons. Those who are ill informed liken it to school glue. You eat it with your fingers. The thicker the poi, the more fingers."

She still did not say anything but just stared through the windshield at the winding road.

"And then you will move on to shark-wrestling."

Still without altering her gaze, but with a slight smile on her lips, she gently moved her hands from her lap, but left his hand lying there so that when she carefully pulled up her skirt, it slid easily between her smooth thighs.

"You are a very, very quick learner," he said, but he was wrong.

❧

Perhaps all that talk about toughening up and wrestling with sharks had had its effect on Anna. She decided that she would try fishing again. She invited Lily along and, at the last minute, Tigger went, too, although she often bragged that even the smell of fish made her "queasy." The captain, Earl Ahanu, and two of his boys waited for them at the wooden pier.

They headed straight out. They were looking for marlin. Lily stood on the ladder to the tower, halfway up, where she could hear her mother laugh quietly when a boy brought them rum in paper cups. Anna was happy.

"But there's no pineapple ring in mine!" Tigger said.

The boy giggled and ran back to his seat on the bow, his bare legs hanging over the sides in the spray.

Tigger said something about the deck boy Lily couldn't quite make out but her mother smiled and shook her head.

"It could be worse," said Tigger.

"Yes," said Anna. "I could be raising pedigreed cocker spaniels." She wore sun-bleached Levi's and a man's white cotton shirt. Lily loved to look at her: she was calm and ferocious at the same time.

"It could be a lot worse, sugar."

The women lowered their voices. At the same time, Earl Ahanu and Lily jumped, certain they had spotted their first sailfish. On circling back, they saw that it was only a dolphin.

"How exciting!" said Tigger. She stood up to watch the dolphin leap back and forth over the wake. "They have been known to have sex with humans."

Anna laughed and the boy refilled their cups from a wicker thermos.

"They never sleep," she said.

"Even Sheridan can't pay them that well," said Tigger.

"The dolphins. They do not have a sympathetic nervous system. They must stay awake in order to breathe. Breathing to them is a conscious action."

Tigger narrowed her eyes and looked up at Lily for confirmation. Lily nodded. "They don't have dolphins in Texas," Tigger said.

Up in the tower, Earl Ahanu smiled. He never took his eyes off the ocean, scanning slowly and carefully back and forth. Lily thought that what would normally be called the whites of his eyes, in Earl's case would be called the yellows of his eyes. When she was little she thought his strange, creamy eyes were what enabled him to find fish. The deck boy was cutting fresh bait. Blood splashed over the wooden boards.

"If you vomit, Tigger, we're putting in," Anna said quietly.

Tigger just looked at her. "You could leave him, you know," she said abruptly. "Just take the kids and go. You could go anywhere. Anywhere in the damn world."

"I wouldn't go to Texas."

"I mean it. And you know it's true yourself. You just won't do it."

Tigger stopped as the boy reset the lines, jerking them against the heavy wake to test the drag.

"I can't," Lily heard her mother say. She started to giggle. "I love him."

"Oh shit," said Tigger.

They were all quiet for a long time. The boys ate their lunch. The women kept drinking. Lily moved up to sit next to Earl Ahanu. He rolled a cigarette and gave her some dried cuttlefish to eat. He was still alert for any sign: circling birds, a floating log, a splash, the splayed taut fin of a great black marlin. But there was nothing. It was very hot. Tigger stretched out on a mat, lying on her stomach, and took off her bikini top. She arched enough so that she could see the back of Anna's head. She was sitting in the fighting chair, staring at the ocean.

"I know you!" Tigger said. "You're not going to do anything about that tramp, are you?"

Anna didn't look around. "Oh, Tigger," she said. She sounded very tired.

"I heard she had some venereal disease or something. At her age."

Anna slowly pivoted the chair around and stared at Tigger.

"I only heard, Nani," said Tigger. She looked frightened.

Anna stood up slowly and with great care, as though she

were an invalid afraid of falling, she walked to the side of the boat and with one quick and graceful movement slid a large emerald off her third finger and dropped it over the side.

"Good Christ!" shouted Tigger. She jumped up, bare-breasted, and rushed to the railing. "Good Christ," she said again, staring into the dense, green water.

Anna looked up at the tower.

"Take her in, Ahanu," she called. "No fish today."

FOUR

ITTLE ANNA wanted nothing in this world so much as a
pair of tap shoes. She talked about them for some time,
wondering out loud whether the black patent were finer than
the red and whether or not they should have buttons or laces.
She worried that we would not be able to find the one pair
that was meant for her. Her view of the world, at five years,
was sufficiently wary to suspect that the tap shoes meant for
her did not exist.

I decided to find them for her, even though it was a risky
business, looking for tap shoes in the middle of the Caribbean.
Tōsi made some inquiries. He received a number of odd
looks but at last he was advised to try a department store in the
capital city. We started out early one sweltering morning,
traveling in a new taxi covered with prohibitive signs, including one forbidding the passenger to look in the driver's
mirror. "Voodoo," I whispered to Tōsi, but he pretended not
to hear. As the representative of a minority, he does not hold
much with religious or racial jokes. It is one of the reasons

we stay only in good hotels. They are more accustomed to idiosyncrasy, but I cannot resist teasing him now and then.

Anna was excited and anxious, her little hand cool inside my big hand. "Do you think we'll find them?" she asked.

"I hope so, darling." I squeezed her hand.

"They'll be there," she said. Magic thinking, I thought, and I began to worry just as Tōsi turned to look at me disapprovingly.

"You're just as bad," I said quietly to him.

He shook his head. "You think you're a sorcerer," he said. "And she's beginning to believe you. Now I'm even hoping we won't find them."

"I'm all she has," I said.

"You say that, but it isn't true. You want it to be that way. Lucky for her, it's only a dream. She has a father, she has grandparents, she has an uncle, she has an aunt, she has friends. She did not spring from your forehead. As you like to believe." He reached over and gently smoothed the top of her wind-blown head. She was leaning out the window.

"My father certainly overeducated you," I said. "I'm sorry," I said just as quickly. He did not answer. I have never been able to bear his disapproval. It shames and infuriates me. The times we have been separated, when my father sent him away and when I left him behind, have been torture for me. I feel incomplete away from him and when he disapproves of me, it is the same feeling: he is not there.

"I have something for you to read," I said and handed him Jessie's letter.

He read it twice, then folded it with his fine, precise (and yes, Japanese, I thought) movements.

"She was always very angry," he said.

"I can't blame her. She's very intelligent, you know."

He smiled. "She doesn't say whether Jack-san is still in India."

"I'm afraid we're going to have to spend even less money now."

"We can manage."

"Yes," I said. We do not have too much money, but we do have a lot of time. In order to conserve, we sacrifice on certain things, like clothes and restaurants and toys and gifts. We have few belongings and we move very leisurely. At first, it was difficult getting used to the sometimes extreme climates, because, for economy, we always travel in the off season. It can be very, very hot in the Caribbean Sea in August. But we are quite adjusted now and no longer take much notice.

Anna ducked her head inside for an instant, saw that we were all right, and disappeared, smiling, back into her hair and the wind.

"Do you remember the cards Jack sent when he went away, the ones I used to send on to you in Tokyo?" Tōsi laughed and nodded. Talking about Jack, with his strange sense of humor, always made Tōsi happy. When Jack ran off and we didn't hear from him for eleven months, the first message he sent to us was on an embossed Christmas card, the kind with a printed greeting, ordered in Kodak camera shops. Usually sent by large families to give their friends an end-of-year update, the sunny amateur photograph decorated at each corner with sprigs of holly or bells, Jack's card showed him perched in a gold howdah on the back of a royal elephant. The laminated message he had chosen was "Good Tidings to All Men." Behind him in the howdah was a grinning Indian bearer holding a rifle with a telescopic sight. After the first astonishment, I was very relieved. I had thought he was in Viet Nam. The second Christmas he was photographed in a jungle setting, dressed rajah-style, with a jeweled dagger in his apple-green cummerbund, his elegantly slippered foot on the head of a dead tiger. The native with the rifle was behind him, still smiling wide-eyed for the photographer. The cards continued for five years, every Christmas, each photograph showing what the year had brought, not in high school diplomas and transfers to company headquarters, but in increased alienation. His humor never left him, although sometimes I worried about his mind.

There were letters in between, witty and irreverent, keeping me up to date on the political problem in Nepal and the difficulty of finding high-grade marijuana in Goa. By the fifth Christmas, he had undergone a different kind of transformation. The card ("Peace on Earth") showed him in a saffron robe, head shaved, each thumb and forefinger held together in a lotus pose. He looked happy. And then the witty letters and Christmas cards stopped.

Instead I received occasional passionate letters about the Hare Krishna movement, often with a reminder that "the Great Lord Krishna knows all." I had not seen my father since I left home, or written to him, but I was so worried about Jack that I wrote to ask whether he could do something to help him. What he did was simply to forward my letter to Jack in Lahore and Jack's letters abruptly stopped. He refused my letters. I had betrayed him, he wrote to Jessie. I was the one who was crazy.

It was only a while ago that he wrote to me again. He was still in India, but hoping to leave. He did not mention the Great Lord Krishna. He had applied to Harvard Law School and expected to hear back from them soon. His letter was funny and smart. He was still Jack. I felt guilty about having worried and worried now that he would become conventional.

"Where do you think he is?" I asked.

Tōsi looked out the window. "Jack?"

"No. Father." I wondered to myself whether it mattered. It was hard after all these years to worry about Sheridan. He was never the kind of person you worried about.

"Do you think he's in Japan?"

"I don't know. Perhaps."

"Those months when you were sent there, when we were little, did you miss us?"

"Yes, I missed you. Of course I missed you. It was difficult. Your father tried to help me."

"But he was the one who sent you. It was his idea."

"You know what he was like. He was interested in the long view. He didn't want me to become too Westernized."

"I suppose he thought it was too late for the rest of us?"

Tōsi laughed. "I think he was mistaken. About many things. But he felt he had this double responsibility to me — to raise me in your family and yet to keep me Japanese."

"I wanted to be Japanese too so that I could be with you. I used to pull my eyes in the mirror."

"I pushed the corners of my eyes in to make them round." His mood changed and he became sad.

"I used to think that you were the only one he ever tried to help." He turned and looked at me strangely. "Somehow he expected the rest of us to just go on. Or not go on." I could feel myself growing angry, the old feelings again.

The taxi finally stopped in front of a big store. Tōsi paid and we went inside.

There were fans on the ceiling and it was a little cooler than in the taxi. We wandered through the store listlessly, looking in every corner. We finally asked a black clerk. He yawned twice and gestured vaguely toward the music section. Like one of Jack's homing pigeons, Anna went straight for them. They were wedged between a snare drum and a rusty cymbal: white tap shoes with red satin ribbons.

Exhausted, we did not get home until dusk. The lights in the bungalow had been turned on and tea was cold on the table. Anna was too excited to eat anything. She ran from room to room, looking for the right place to try out the shoes, but the tiles were uneven or there was matting on the floors.

"We'll go outside," I said. So she ran out to the driveway, the tap shoes in a big plastic shopping bag, and we followed her, only now the cook was behind us too, waiting to see the famous shoes.

Anna sat in the grass by the side of the drive and I helped her put them on. It was almost dark. The white shoes looked enormous at the ends of her long, skinny legs. I tied the red satin bows several times before she thought the knots were beautiful enough. The shoes looked like court pumps Louis XIV might have worn.

She stood up carefully, arms outspread for balance. Shaking off my helping hand, she stepped onto the hard-top. Tōsi watched from the path in front of the bungalow, silhouetted by the golden light coming from the open door.

Anna stood there. She looked down at her feet for a long, long time. She did not move. She glanced up at me quickly, inquiringly, then stared down again at the huge white shoes, which seemed to shine in the deepening twilight. She was very still and quiet, as though she were listening and waiting. Finally, she looked up. Her eyes were full of tears.

"They don't work," she said very quietly. I did not know what she meant at first. I must have looked bewildered, because she said again, wise and defeated, "These shoes don't work."

She turned away, toward the house, and before I could stop her she awkwardly clicked and clacked her way inside, not even looking at Tōsi as she stumbled past. The shoes were silenced abruptly when she stepped through the doorway onto the mat and she disappeared into the light like a ghost.

Sometimes in the night I wake and go into Anna's room and bend over her and watch her. She does not sleep tucked into herself, rounded, but flung out, violently, as though she has been dropped onto the bed from above. Her mouth is open and shining wet and the thumb that has slipped out at the moment of sleep lies a few inches from her face, fingers curled, thumb cocked.

I want to stay with her. I want to get into bed with her. The back of her neck will be damp with perspiration, and as she senses my body next to hers, she will move and sigh and throw her arm across me. I know because I have done this many nights, slipped in beside her and watched her sleep and thought about things. I am afraid that something is going to happen to her. I am afraid that she will die. But if I am there, lying next to her, able at any moment to shield her body with my own, everything will be all right. But I force myself out of her room and back down the long corridor to my own bed.

Tōsi is right. In my heart, I have always thought of her as only my child, fatherless, miraculously conceived. Even when I was pregnant and I insisted on referring to the child inside me as "she," the doctor wearily cautioned that it was impossible to know its sex.

But when this girl was finally born and the doctor, shaking his head in wonder, said "Let's go to Las Vegas," I did not feel any special pleasure in being right. I was past that. I was already in her dark room, bending over the bed where she lay akimbo, as though dropped from a great height.

I now had what I wanted. I too believed in magic thinking and had become both my own mother and my own daughter. We did not need a father. Fathers were dangerous. In this triangle there could be no man. It was a struggle between three females. I would become the good mother and prove that I was not big Anna, and I would become the loved child that was little Anna, at long last loved safely by the good mother. If I could make Anna happy, then I would be free of the wicked spell. Perhaps in my devotion to Anna, I would forget my mother.

Rooted to nothing but the thought of undoing the enchantment, bound to no place and no thing but Anna, I wander about the world, stopping here and there, giving up Anna to her father when I must, for that is part of being a good mother too, suffering when she is out of my sight, even for a day.

I realize now that I have fallen into an awful trap, set by myself. This Anna does not free me from the ghost of the other Anna. Nor should she have the burden of such a morbid task. Just as I once felt fused to my mother, so I have fused my daughter to myself. As I once grew frantic if my mother was too long gone from a room, so I now fret and pace if Anna is fifteen minutes late from the park. My mother made herself too important in my life, involved me too deeply, and I am doing the same thing to Anna. Binding myself to the one will not free me from the other. I am doing exactly what I blame my mother for doing. I must stop. This idea of doing, undoing, doing again, is all wrong. My daughter is not my mother. I am not my mother.

FIVE

$\mathscr{F}$OR THREE HOURS every afternoon, even in summer, except when Tōsi was away, Sheridan gave lessons to Lily and Tōsi in his big library. Tōsi worked for an hour with him alone, then Lily joined them. They studied Japan. They were good students and Sheridan was a good teacher. They sat cross-legged on mats with small ebony writing tables in front of them. Surrounded by exquisite objects of every kind, Sheridan encouraged them to handle sharp samurai swords and rare bronze heads smuggled out of the north of Japan and seventeenth-century celadon teacups. Lily sometimes daydreamed, staring out the narrow space between the wooden shutter doors, watching the sky, listening always for Anna's movements in the old, dry house. As serious as he was about these lessons, Sheridan never called her back when he noticed her daydreaming but allowed her to fly off and return on her own. The lessons were very pleasant. Tōsi studied with a formality that was sometimes irritating to Lily, who saw this special time spent with Sheridan as a lovely treat. But Tōsi seemed to know something that Lily could only sense, that the lessons were, apart from his own private study, and perhaps his patients at the hospital, the most thrilling part of her father's day.

As they were about to finish one rainy afternoon, Lily heard Anna coming along the verandah. Anna never came in during the lessons. No one ever interrupted them. Something must be wrong, Lily thought immediately. But Anna was smiling, her face flushed and wet with rain as she noisily pushed the doors wider apart and came into the peaceful room, not bothering to wipe her feet. Lily smiled at Tōsi, and Sheridan looked at his watch.

"I need to speak to you," she said to him. She had seen his gesture. She seemed giddy. Lily knew Anna was supposed to be at her Japanese flower-arranging class in town. It went through Lily's mind that the entire household, including the servants in their gray house kimonos with white obis, was devoted to serving her father's interests. For one rebellious moment she wondered what they received in return, but the notion of her father's benign protection was so strong that she quickly felt guilty for having such an ungrateful thought.

"All right, children," he said, tenderly rolling up a Hokusai. Tōsi and Lily put away their writing materials. Lily watched Anna sideways. She wished she could stay to listen. Anna didn't seem to notice that Tōsi and Lily were there. She came farther into the room.

"I've been thinking a lot about suffering," she said abruptly. She pulled a chair away from the desk but she did not sit down.

Tōsi caught Lily's eye with a quick look of alarm as they went out. Lily looked back over her shoulder. Her mother was standing next to the chair, squeezing the hem of her dress, unaware that she was making a puddle, while her father fondly put away his scrolls and books. Lily decided to climb the mango tree in the yard; she would not be able to hear them, but she would be able to see when her mother came out. She beckoned to Tōsi to follow her up the tree, but he shook his head, looking shocked, and disappeared into the house. He was against spying.

Anna watched Lily climb the tree, framed in the big, open window, but she did not really see her. She shook her head when Sheridan motioned to her to sit down, reminding her by his politeness that she was, after all, a guest in his room. She did not sit down, but watched him as he gracefully put jade daggers and carved ivory monkeys back into red-silk-lined boxes.

"You seem upset," he said quietly, his back turned to her for a moment.

"Well, yes," she said. "I think I am."

He sat down on a big, soft sofa and lit a cigarette and handed it to her. Because he was tall, his legs went under a table and out one side, and when she began to walk back and forth before him, she had to step over his shins once or twice, before he politely tucked them under the table.

"I have thought two things about you, more than two things, of course, but two things lately seem to stay in my mind," she said nervously. She did not give him his usual chance to be amused, but quickly went on. "It seems to me that having observed suffering, even terrible suffering, as you have, that having been through that, it does not then entitle you to judge all other suffering by that one terrible standard. There are many horrible things in the world, each with its own awfulness." She stopped, afraid she was not making sense, but when she saw that he was paying attention, not fiddling or looking at his hands, she continued, only calmer now and more assured.

"I know that you are famous for being a compassionate man. Very famous. And that you are invited to give talks on kindness." She smiled at the thought. "I cannot remember the formal title." He smiled too.

" 'Seminars on the Agony of War Survival,' " he said. "It doesn't matter," he added quickly.

"Well, it does matter, in a way, because you are good at it, not just famous because you know about it, but famous because you did it, you were there."

"The funny thing," he said quietly, "is that it was never intentional. I certainly had no wish to be famous. Worse than that, I had no particular interest in being 'kind,' as you put it."

"But you were. You must have been the first American they saw. You had medicine. They died in your arms. And you took the child."

"They spit at me too. Only one or two, though, were still possessed of that kind of logic. I was angrier, I suppose, than they were."

"They would not have had the time or strength to be angry," she said, as if she knew.

"Yes," he said. He suddenly sounded weary and she frowned slightly as she realized that she might already be losing his attention. She had not yet said what she had come to tell him.

"What I am trying to say," she went on quickly, "is that what you saw there became your definition of suffering. And mere human, everyday suffering means nothing to you."

He looked at her curiously, as if it had suddenly occurred to him that she might be intelligent. She was very beautiful, too, in the yellow afternoon light. Her awkwardness and her wetness made her look very young.

"And to tell you the truth," she said hurriedly, "it makes me furious when you receive all those invitations to 'Congresses on Compassion' and — "

He interrupted her by laughing. In answer to her worried look, he said, "You're very witty sometimes."

"Thank you very much." She took a step closer to him. He was now half lying on the sofa, his head lolled back against a cushion. He motioned with his head for her to come beside him, so delicately that someone who did not know him well would have missed the suggestion. It was very tempting to her and just as she felt her body begin to slide weightlessly toward him and saw from under her half-closed lids his own eyes closing, she held herself back. She clasped and unclasped her hands in front of her and saw that now he was the one to frown.

"What I am trying to say is that I do not think you are especially kind. I think you are honest when you say it was a question of circumstance." She stopped to breathe. She was amazed at herself and afraid. She waited for him to rise impatiently and stretch and walk away, but he only said, "There is something more you want to say."

As she watched his handsome, grave face, his gray eyes looking at her with both mockery and admiration, she wondered for an instant whether she might be making a mistake. "Please tell me about the girl," she blurted out suddenly, before she could change her mind and ease down onto him on the sofa, the way he wanted her to. "The Filipino who works at the hospital."

"Filipina," he said, jumping up. She realized that the conversation was over, that she had lost him, but she refused to give up.

"That girl called Christmas."

"There is nothing to tell, Anna. She is very young. Sometimes she helps in my wing. Delivering specimens, picking up breakfast trays." He went to the window and stuck his head out, looking for more rain. Lily was no longer in the tree.

"Why does everyone say things then? About the two of you."

"I don't know. I am kind to her. That word again. We will have to think of another." He sighed and turned back to the room. "She says her parents beat her, and sometimes she is badly bruised when she comes to work."

"Perhaps she deserves it."

"I don't know," he said. He walked over to turn the desk chair back into its place. She was frozen in regret and could not move aside when his easy body brushed against her stiff one. He looked at her absent-mindedly and brushed back the dark hair where it had dried in curls on her face. She tried to stop his hand at her cheek, but it was too late; he had already begun to turn away.

She let his hand go and he was gone.

"Is that it?" she called after him. "Class dismissed?" she yelled, but there was no one to hear her.

⌒❦

In the days after, when her mother retired to her large, pretty rooms and closed the big paneled doors behind her, Lily felt very nervous. Lily always felt unsettled when her mother was not around. It was not enough that she was in the house: it was important that Lily *see* her. So Lily wandered anxiously through the house, which in turn distracted her father and he advised her to find something to do. After having read every book she had borrowed from the school library, she had the idea to copy the Gospel of St. Mark into her diary. She copied it before and after her Japan lessons and sometimes in the night, standing at a bureau next to the window, writing on the top of the bureau so that she could watch the verandah outside Anna's rooms.

She had written out several chapters, not realizing how

close to dinner it was, when Tōsi came to tell her that Anna wanted to see her. When she didn't put down her pen immediately, he said, "You better, missy." She lay the pen down dramatically, wondering whether Tōsi believed for one minute that she wouldn't run whenever her mother called.

"You'll ruin your eye, anyway," he said importantly.

"Eyes," she said and brushed out past him.

Although it was just twilight, her mother was sitting up in her bed in a pale, lime satin nightdress. The room was cool and dark, shaded and refreshed by the great wild vines that snaked through the unscreened windows. Despite her voluptuousness, Anna looked chaste and girlish, like a young nun.

"Hi, darling," she said. She was very cheerful. Not at all like someone who has been in her room for two days, Lily thought. "I am sorry to take you away from Nancy Drew and the Mysterious Case of the Disappearing Mother."

"I was copying something from the New Testament," Lily said.

"You were?" Anna said, not really paying attention. Lily sat on the edge of the bed and noticed, in the dim light, six big, yellow grapefruit lined up on the bedside table.

"Are you feeling goofy?" Lily asked.

"Do I look goofy?"

That was their code word. It more or less meant verging out of control. They had picked it out the year before and saved it for those infrequent, at least recently infrequent, times when Anna felt herself slipping away. If she whispered "goofy" to Lily at a tea party it meant that Lily was to take her home immediately.

"No, not really." Lily had trained herself, drilled herself really, in the careful distinction between irrational and eccentric. Lily had no intention of ever failing Anna, but this

55

time Anna seemed fine. A little mischievous perhaps. Another secret, Lily thought with loyal resignation, another awful secret to hear.

"I need your help." Anna smiled conspiratorily. Lily was not surprised. As always, Anna was irresistible.

"I suppose it has something to do with these grapefruit?"

"Do not be ironic, my old sweetheart. Or is it facetious? You never learned that from me."

"Please don't be mean to me," Lily said quietly.

Anna looked down at her hands, folded in luxurious piety on top of the cool linen sheets.

"Not mean," she said gravely. "Maybe a little hysterical. That's all." She looked up and smiled tentatively.

"What do you want me to do?"

"Well!" she said, suddenly gay again. She opened the drawer of her table and carefully took out a white lace mantilla. It was wrapped loosely around something. She laid it gently on her lap.

"I want to teach you . . ." She slowly unfolded the mantilla. Inside was an old yellow newspaper and wrapped inside the newspaper were two syringes. She picked one up delicately and dipped the point of the needle into the water carafe on the table, drawing back the plunger.

"Where did you get those?" Lily whispered.

"Mister Big-Shot-Doctor-Nobel-Prize-Nominee," she said.

"Father?" Lily whispered.

Her mother held the syringe up to the light and squirted out the air bubbles with a sudden high spray of water. "Ooops," she said playfully. "That part is very important. You could kill someone." She held the syringe vertically in one hand, her thumb resting expertly on the plunger, and picked up a grapefruit, cradling it like a skull in the other hand.

Lily could hear Jack and Jessie being called to dinner. She

decided to ignore her mother. She reached inside the mantilla, casually laying aside the other syringe, and took out the old newspaper. It cracked as she carefully unfolded it. It was the *Bryn Mawr Times,* dated May 1942. Lily had to search for a few minutes until she found, amidst the announcements of USO entertainments and war-bond parties given by society ladies, a small article about the forthcoming marriage of Captain Sheridan Shields and a pretty debutante named Virginia Butler, whose father was a senator. There was a photograph of the young couple. Lily read that Mrs. Dixon Shields was giving a small dance (small in keeping with the war effort) at home, for her only son and his fiancée.

"But that's Father," Lily said. She looked at her mother for an explanation.

"Yes. And that is not me."

"But who was this person?" Lily asked. She was shocked.

"He should have married her," Anna said without spite. "They were really very well suited." She watched Lily with amusement.

"But what about you? How did this happen?" Lily pointed insistently to the newspaper article.

"His mother liked her very much."

"Grandmother?"

"Oh, yes," Anna said, "that's right. Your grandmother. I always forget that you are related to her."

"I don't know very much about Father."

"There is not much to know. There never is. I don't mean about him, but about anybody, about me. I was eighteen years old, Catholic, Irish and very poor, the daughter of a ladies' maid, someone who would have worked for her. She refused to see me when he took me home."

"She sees you now," Lily said. Her voice was full of hope.

Anna shrugged. "I thought of her while I was here in bed

the last few days. Funny if I turned out to be like her. Now, she had a very interesting solution: she decided one day never to walk again."

Lily had never heard any of this. She thought she knew everything about Anna, but this was a new story. She curled her legs up under herself like a pet, like the child she was, settling in front of the fire for a fairy tale.

"One day when your father was a young boy, he was eating a green apple in the music room of his parents' house. They were very rich, you see. They had special rooms for things like music — or sunlight. He had taken one bite when he heard a strange, fluttering sound, like a bird trapped inside, and he rushed from room to room, somehow knowing that the sound was important. He found his mother, rustling in her taffeta dressing gown, on the floor. She was paralyzed from the waist down. And your father grew up believing, convinced, that she could walk if she only wanted to walk. His father took her to all the doctors, who confirmed her condition, but your father never, ever believed it."

"And my grandfather?"

"Oh, he devoted his life to her and died very young." Anna smiled wickedly. "He bought hospitals, you know, as a hobby. That is how I met Sheridan. At one of the hospitals. I had just gone into nursing and he had come to see his father about something, because he refused to work himself in any of his father's hospitals. Seeing as how he owned about a hundred, it is probably why Sheridan always ended up in such odd places. It seemed so strange to me. To begin with, I never knew until then that one person could *own* a hospital, go out and *buy* a hospital. Such an eerie thing to want." She shook her head, both at the notion of buying hospitals and the futility of ever understanding behavior. She turned the grapefruit around in her hand and looked tenderly at Lily.

"There may come a time, my old sweetheart," she said abruptly, "when I may not be able to do this myself." She was wide-eyed and elated again. Anna overturned the grapefruit into her daughter's hand.

"So I want you to practice."

Some days that summer when Lily could not stand it any longer and was exhausted by her attempts to make sense out of it, she would wait and watch by Anna's side until the drugs had taken their effect and her mother had fallen asleep or into a mild, but open-eyed, stupor. Then she would sneak out of the still house and scuttle sideways down the long coral drive like a crab, watchful and eager not to be seen. On these days, she knew she had a few hours before Anna was herself again.

What was difficult was that some days, and sometimes even for days in a row, Anna was perfectly fine. It would have been better for Lily had Anna simply been one way or the other. It would have been a certainty, a condition, and Lily could have rearranged her life to accommodate it. But this way, there was no knowing. To wake every morning was to be dry-mouthed and sick with anxiety until she could run across the house to Anna's rooms. Often she knew before she got there from the expression on a maid's face or an ambush by a pale Tōsi whether or not Mrs. Anna was goofy.

Lily was the only one allowed to handle her. Often when she came in the morning she noticed that her father had already been there. Sometimes he would forget (or perhaps not forget) his black medical bag on a chair near the bed. Once, Lily had kicked the heavy bag off the chair and millions, it seemed to her millions, of pills and packets and hypodermic needles had rolled into the corners. She had stayed away the whole day and when she returned someone had cleaned up

59

the mess and the bag had disappeared. She never knew who did it.

She would sit with her mother until some time near noon, when Anna grew giggly and sleepy. When she had made sure by various homemade tests that Anna would not notice, she would back out of the room on tiptoe and sneak out of the house. She did not tiptoe and creep for her mother's sake. She could easily have moved around the room in snowshoes — it would not have bothered Anna — but she did not want anyone else to know she was leaving the house. Not that she was going anyplace special. She just needed something, even an hour or two, for herself.

She walked down the road to the palm-frond windbreak where the bus waited at the end of the line. The palm branches were old and dry and did not stop the wind coming damp and salty across the king's fishpond. Men in small boats, waiting for mullet, floated on the flat, silver pond, and the Koolau Range rose black and green above the valley. Sometimes the bus was already there, but usually she waited, her thin skirt flapping in the wind, her bare feet in the stiff marsh grass. It was very calming for her. She rode the bus line back and forth.

It was a forty-minute ride to the first shopping center. The shopping center had a supermarket, a bakery and a swimming-pool showroom. The showroom had nothing in it, but Scotch-taped to the walls were cutouts of pool shapes — kidney beans and circles and even hearts.

When she jumped off the bus there, she went first to the bakery and bought a custard-filled pastry called a Long John. The Samoan woman wrapped it in waxed paper and sullenly passed it to her over the display case. Lily sat on the curb outside, facing the big, empty parking lot, and ate it slowly. Sometimes she forgot about the powdered sugar and breathed too quickly, sucking in the sugar, which made her cough hard once or twice. She looked around to see whether the woman in the bakery had noticed, but she was not there.

For Lily it was exhilarating to be alone. No one knew where she was, no one needed her, and if they did, they could not find her. She had a little bit of money. It was hot. It was early afternoon. She stood up, casually brushed the sugar off her legs and strolled slowly, even carelessly, to the bus stop to begin the next part of her journey.

It was thirty more minutes to Kaimuki, a small town on the top of a hill with saimin stalls and dry-goods stores. Sometimes she jumped off there. The town was old, founded by Japanese immigrants. The tiny shops and tiny houses were made of wood. Vanda orchids grew in the lush front yards. Women hobbled along in kimonos and getas, clacking on the narrow sidewalks, smiling at her shyly as they turned in at their gates or shop doors shaded with long, floating strips of printed cotton.

Sometimes Lily went into the shops, dark and cool, which smelled like the inside of a cedar chest, and she would glide peacefully down the narrow dusty aisles, dragging her hand lightly over stacked bolts of cloth, twirling her fingers through glass wind chimes, dust motes and tinkling notes set off together in the still air. An old Japanese man, bowlegged and barefoot, once peered around a corner, curious and toothless, and she was grateful he did not speak to her. She did not want to talk.

She wondered what they were doing at home: Mother is just waking. The children are playing. Mother is still in her nightgown. Tōsi looks for me and cannot find me. Mother asks whether the mail has arrived, and they tell her it hasn't, not until three. She wanders back to her room.

Lily looked at the Japanese dolls in the glass cases on the

top shelves, with their thick red and gold brocade obis and intricate heavy wigs stuck through with silk cherry blossoms and silver butterflies. These dolls are for admiring, she thought. Girls could not play with these dolls. Their bisque faces were beautiful, with painted lidless eyes and tiny, peaked, melancholy mouths, erotic and passive: Mother thinks about getting dressed but decides to wait until the letter from her mother arrives with the post. Jack walks his bicycle up the hill to the pigeon coop. Tōsi still looks for me. Jessie counts and straightens her toys again.

It was another forty minutes to the old hotel downtown. It was a businessman's hotel. There were no tourists downtown and not many women or children. The streets with names like Beretania and Bougainvillea were cool, shaded by the two- and three-story wooden buildings with offices above street-level shops. Near the port, there were tattoo parlors and bars and young sailors who wandered up and down talking to brown girls lounging barefoot against signposts. Lily was not allowed to go down those streets, called River Street and Hotel Street, with the teen-age servicemen and jukeboxes, but knew she must stay on the main road, which ran by the old palace and the park with the filigreed bandstand. There was a lunch wagon behind the park and men waited in line for teriyaki and cole slaw on white cardboard plates. They ate standing under trees or carried their plates into the park. On Wednesday afternoons the Royal Band, old men in red tunics and crisp white trousers, played for an hour in the bandstand. They played old native waltzes and Polynesian love songs in march time. The music was sharp and sad. Lily sat in the grass in the open light until the musicians finished, fat and sighing in their immaculate, stiff uniforms. When they began to pull apart the brass instruments and lay the sections in velvet-lined cases, she got up and headed back to the bus.

There were some days when she didn't even get off the bus. The drivers recognized her and nodded without smiling. Sometimes, at the end of the line, they did not charge her the return fare. She always sat by the back door in case she decided to get off quickly. She always opened the window. In the late afternoons, when the bus was crowded, she had to share the seat. Sometimes on the way back, she saw someone she knew, someone who worked on the plantation, but she kept her head turned to the window, the wind blowing the skin of her face taut and smooth. She did not look at anyone.

She thought always of home: now Jack and Jessie lie on their beds, on clean white cotton blankets, on their stomachs. Lips open and close. Saliva is swallowed. Eyes close in afternoon sleep. The windows are wide open, curtainless, screenless, and the smell of flowers weaves in and out of their hair, hair that is dry at first, but grows damp as they fall deeper into sleep.

The bus reached the end of the line just as it was getting dark and Lily walked back up the winding road to the Big House. The mynah birds were quiet in the banyans as she passed. Small bats dived over the cane. A fisherman with huge, black, splayed feet passed near her. He frightened her for a moment because she did not see him until he was right beside her. When she reached the house, she could hear the record of jazz violin that her mother played every day. She could hear the song "In a Sentimental Mood." Lily knew the record by heart, as did everyone by then. It was Duke Ellington and Stéphane Grappelli. Anna played it quite loud.

The lights were just being turned on. Lily stood in the trees by the side of the drive, in the gray and pink light, watching the old wooden house, letting the high, sad music stream over her into the cooling air. When it was particularly still, she could make out other sounds through the music. A shutter was closed in a child's bedroom, the telephone rang once, rice pots clanged in the kitchen.

She waited under the dripping trees and listened and watched until it was dark and the house was brighter and noisier, with children called for baths and coverlets turned down and evening dresses laid out on beds. She heard Tōsi calling her from the back verandah and because she did not want to worry him she made herself go inside.

As she ran up the stairs, the music stopped suddenly and her feet squeaked on the wood, startling her, stillness all around, until, with a loud scratch, the jazz violin began again and she went to comb her tree-wet hair for dinner.

One night, Anna came into the playroom and sat alongside the children's table, her chair turned sideways to the table, and watched them eat, talking all the while, foolish and flushed, making them laugh. They were a little embarrassed because she was trying so hard.

She was very thin. Her low soft breasts looked shrunken and Lily thought about putting chunks of meat into the deep cavity where the bones met at her throat. It sounded as if she were singing, she spoke so quickly, stopping only for shallow, laughing breaths, timid and fidgety, crossing and changing her legs.

Sheridan came in with a cocktail and leaned against the back of an old armchair, his body indicating that he would not be staying long. Anna went out and came back with a notepad and pencil. She moved and spoke with strange efficiency. She cleared her throat. The children were eating fish and looked up, alerted by her suddenly deliberate movements. Sheridan lit a cigarette and looked out at the mountains. "Well," she said primly. "Anna," he said, not turning to look at her, the cigarette smoke hanging low over the table.

"Well," she said again, "I am glad we are all here together, because I have some very, very important business to conduct." She sat down and crossed her thin legs and flipped open the notebook, balancing it on her knee. She twirled the tip of the pencil between her lips to moisten the lead. Her eyes were very bright. Lily looked at her father. He watched the summer rain clouds moving slowly down over the mountains, blown from the northeast, from the cold Aleutians. Perhaps he hates her, Lily thought, vomits at the sight of her, and wishes she were dead, as I sometimes wish she were dead, as she must wish even more, because just then she said, "When I am dead, I want you children to know that certain things of mine are yours."

Lily, too, looked at the mountains. Jessie let her fork fall from her hand. It clanged on the plate. She sighed loudly and pushed back her chair. It did not stop Anna.

"Lily, my oldest child, my first baby girl, I want you to have the rubies and the gold dress from Venice and—"

It seemed to Lily that Anna was waiting for an interruption, anticipatory, eager even, but she jumped and pretended to be startled when Sheridan finally stood up and turned to look at her. He was frowning, but both of them were formal and polite. What they really want, Lily thought, is to bite through each other's neck and sever the head from the body.

"I'm not finished," Anna said very quietly.

Jack had not stopped eating, nervous and ravenous, although he never ate very much. He noisily slid Jessie's untouched plate onto his own greasy, empty plate and stuffed his mouth with rice, not holding his fork correctly, but gripping it in his fist. Jessie did not notice. She was the only one who looked directly at Anna.

"Let the children have their dinner," Sheridan said. He walked around to the back of her chair. She watched him carefully. She looked as though she were his secretary, taking dictation, waiting attentively while he thought of the next sentence.

"You're not going to die," he said. For a moment it seemed as if she would write it down. He took her hand. She fought him at first, pulling against his grip, her eyes wild and bright, before she pulled herself straight up, against his resistance. The notebook slid to the floor. She looked frightened.

"Let her stay," Lily whispered to him. Sheridan and Anna both turned back to the table.

"I can hardly stand it," Lily whispered.

"You'll always be my babies," Anna said. She started to cry. He left the room.

"I used to think," she said, "that being a mother was different. Different from what I think now." She paused to fight her confusion, then began again, calmer and no longer crying. "Once when I was little, I fell out of a second-story window. My mother jumped out after me and broke both legs. I just laughed and rolled over in the grass. I was not hurt. I remember it felt wonderful when I was falling." She looked at each of the children in turn. They stared at her raptly, adoringly, as if they were memorizing her.

"Anyway," she said, suddenly shy, "I do not think that way anymore. I think that often, most of the time, maybe all of the time, the child gets hurt, too."

She smiled, although she looked sadder than they had ever

seen her. She walked backward to the door, as though she wanted to keep them in sight for as long as possible.

❧

In the middle of the night Lily was awakened by the feeling that someone was in her room. It was very dark. There was no moon. The door had been opened and a thin line of yellow light shone from the lantern at the end of the hall. She turned over quietly, onto her back, and listened. The house was still. It would be hours before the fighting cocks hidden in the cane began to crow. There was a tug on her blanket.

On her hands and knees, at the side of the bed, was her mother. Now Lily could smell her. She leaned over the side, their faces very close, as her eyes opened and shut, trying to make Anna out, trying to make sure that she was not dreaming.

"Mama?" Lily asked in a whisper. She reached out and touched her face. She felt her ear and hair.

"Yes."

"Mama, what are you doing?" Lily sat up.

"Don't turn on the light. Just come with me. I need you to help me."

"Where's Papa?"

"I can't walk," she said. Lily got out at the bottom of the bed so as not to knock her over. She slipped her arms around her mother's waist and turned her around and guided and dragged her like an animal, like a big, dumb puppy, out of her room and down the hall to her own room. It was easier to pull her in the hall because of the smooth mats. Lily could almost slide her. She was goofy, just coming out of it maybe, fighting the drugs. Shaking her head like a puppy, too. Lily was out of breath. Anna wasn't heavy, but she wasn't helping

67

much. They heaved and slid into Anna's room. The lights were on. The sheets on Sheridan's side of the bed were smooth and tucked in. Lily closed the door behind them with her foot.

"Do you think you can get up on the bed?" she whispered.

Anna slowly shook her head back and forth. Suddenly, Lily hated her. She wanted to kick her, like the dog she was, helpless and pathetic and dumb. Dumb of speech and thought, a mess, and dragging Lily into it, all out of control and dripping onto the floor. Get up, she wanted to shout. Anna was still on her hands and knees. She didn't even know to sit up. Maybe I could teach her to do tricks and beg, Lily thought.

"Get up!" Lily shouted.

Anna just looked at her, her head between her shoulders, neckless. Lily started to cry and locked her arms around Anna's chest, under her damp armpits, and heaved and pulled her onto the bed. She fell on top of Lily. They lay there like lovers, legs entwined, sweating, tangled and depleted, without thought. Lily wasn't even crying. They lay like that a long time. Lily thought she must have fallen asleep, but when she eased herself out from under her and came around the bed, she saw that her mother's eyes were open and clear.

"Are you all right?" Lily asked.

"Yes. Are you?"

Lily laugh d shyly and shrugged her shoulders. Anna pulled her nightgown down and covered herself. "I want you to find him," she said.

She patted the edge of the bed for Lily to sit down but Lily stayed where she was, just outside the circle of light from the little reading lamp on Anna's table. She saw on the table pill bottles and the book *Justine*. Anna saw her looking at the table.

"In that book, Justine and her friend stop their car to pick

68

up a box in the middle of the road. They drive on to a party and do not bother to look inside the box until later. When they do, they find a dead baby."

"You'd think they'd have opened it," Lily said, pretending not to be interested. She did not like to encourage Anna when the subject turned to dead babies or stray animals.

"When you were very little," she went on, "you came into the bathroom where I had just miscarried into the toilet. Your father was holding the tiny, barely formed foetus in his hands, but it was running through his fingers. You just stood there. I was trying to baptize it. Do you remember?"

"No," she lied.

"Please sit next to me. I will be all right now. Just sit here a minute and then you can go."

Lily sat on the edge of the bed and they held hands.

"We will go into town tomorrow," Anna said. "Go to the bookstore and pick up Tigger and go to lunch and spend some money. Okay?"

Lily smiled and nodded.

"Little optimisms," Anna said. "A whole day of little optimisms." She squeezed Lily's hand and let go and said in a quick and serious voice, "Will you call him? I know where he is."

Lily didn't answer. She turned away from her. She always surprises me, Lily thought, just when I think it's safe, when it's all right to come out of hiding and run for base. "Why?" she asked, looking down.

"Because I want him to know that I know. He is with that girl. Christmas. The one who works at the hospital. The one with the pretty eyes." She laughed horribly.

"Oh, I couldn't," Lily said. She was terrified. Why is she telling me this? she thought. It is terrible. This is terrible.

"Please. For me. I will never ask you again."

"Yes, you will."

"Please."

"He'll be back," Lily said, pleading.

"I have the number. Tōsi got it for me." She was calm and businesslike.

"Then get Tōsi to call for you."

"Please. I want you to do it."

"It's *awful!*" Lily said loudly. She was moaning.

"Sssh. Come on now. I promise I will never ask you again."

Then Lily heard the sound of a car on the coral drive, way down at the bottom, a crunching sound beyond the poinciana trees, a heavy car, his car.

"There!" she shouted and ran from the room and down the hall as fast as she could go, soundless and swift, as if she were flying. She was in her bed, lying stiff and motionless, heart beating in her neck, before his car even reached the house.

Unexpectedly, a week later, a black Cadillac limousine came up the driveway and stopped under the porte-cochère. The housemaids, hoping for the territorial governor, or his wife at least, hurriedly shook out the tapa floor mats and dusted the Victorian koa-wood furniture dating from the time of Queen Liliuokalani, but to their disappointment it was only Anna in a white dress who walked down the mats, ran her fingers slowly over the heavy sideboards (not testing for dust but out of love and remembrance) and stepped into the bright light slanting onto the verandah. She went down the steps and slid quickly into the back of the car. She did not seem to notice the driver, who stood there politely, holding the door. She did not look back. She seemed to be humming to herself.

Alerted by the arrival of a strange car, the children lined up on the verandah just in time to see their father come down the steps and get into the car, next to Anna. They waved good-bye as the doors fell closed heavily and the car crackled around the drive. Anna turned to wave vaguely from the back window, as though she were leaving on an ocean liner, unable to make out the faces in the dockside crowd. They stood there long after the car vanished into the trees, the younger children waiting for an explanation from Lily.

"She's gone," Jack said. "Fishing, I think."

Lily didn't answer. Jessie plucked blossoms from the lilikoi vine, snapping them noisily from their stems and dropping the bruised flowers onto her pink feet. "Something's wrong," said Lily. Jessie snorted in contempt. Jessie was always a good gauge of doom. Lily admired Jessie's instinct for trouble.

"It's not fish," Jessie said.

They realized, late that night, that their mother was not coming home. Jack and Jessie lay disconsolate and stupefied on Lily's bed. Lily lay on the bare floor and watched the purple summer sky through the open French doors. The offshore breeze had died down and the sound of the sea with it. There were no curtains to hide the cloudless sky, and Lily was thinking: My mother did not like curtains in her house, my mother does not like curtains in her house, my mother will not like curtains in her house.

Tōsi tiptoed into the room. Lily was very relieved to see him. She had not seen him all day and she had been anxiously looking for him. Her father had come back late in the afternoon and gone immediately to his library, with instructions that he was not to be disturbed.

Jack and Jessie barely looked up when Tōsi came in. They had already told Lily that they were not moving, that from now on they were sleeping with her in her bed, every night.

Lily rolled onto her side as Tōsi kneeled down next to her excitedly and pulled a folded piece of white paper from his shirt. He handed it to her.

"From Anna-san," he said quietly. Jack jumped off the bed. Jessie took her fingers out of her mouth. Lily sat up and slowly unfolded the paper, both afraid and happy about what she might find there. She looked at Tōsi for a clue, but he shook his head and said, "She told me to give it to you and you would read it to us." Lily stood up and went to the French doors, where she could face the garden, her back to the others.

She read aloud, " 'My sweet children,' " then she stopped as her eyes raced ahead, eager for information, until Jack shouted, "Lily, out loud, read it to us!"

" 'My sweet children. I am going away for a few days, perhaps a few weeks, because I am not well. I am not sick, so you must not worry, but I am not as well as I should be, or rather, as well as I want to be. When I come back I will be my old self. I told your father I was writing to you. I will miss you so much. I wish you could visit, but you are not allowed to see patients. Love and hundreds of kisses, Mama. Lily, do not let Jessie go to the Point by herself and make sure Jack takes his medicine.' " Lily stopped. She noticed that the writing paper had been torn from a child's notebook. Anna had written the note in a hurry.

"Is that all?" Jack asked quietly.

"There's a whole row of X's and O's. Hugs and kisses." Lily was looking into the dark garden. She had made things as perfect as she could for her mother. More was not possible, but still she had left them. Tōsi came up next to her and she handed him the note without looking at him. She heard them all like an echo, like in the Wet Cave.

"I wish we knew where she was," Jack said. "I mean which place. They wouldn't let us in, I know, but we could always wait outside and watch and maybe we'd see her in the window or something." He was twisting his hands.

"If she says she is coming back, she is," said Tōsi. He sounded angry. He put the letter into Lily's hand and stepped through the doors and disappeared into the darkness outside. They listened to the dry leaves caught beneath his feet crack into small pieces.

"Part of me feels like hating her," Jessie said.

Lily went to sit with them on the small bed. "Did you take your medicine today?" she asked Jack. He shook his head.

"She'll be back," Lily said sadly. Jessie sighed heavily and pulled the light coverlet over herself. Jack went obediently to take his medicine, thrilled to be doing something for Anna, and Lily stretched herself out on the floor again. Her bones felt hot and stiff. She wondered what had happened to make Anna finally leave them behind. She speculated long and tirelessly through the night. Long after Jessie had fallen asleep and Jack had come back and lain down next to Jessie on the bed and Tōsi had stopped moaning and rustling in the trees, she was still wondering what she might have done to drive her mother away.

A few days after the children had settled in Lily's small room for good, Sheridan came in unexpectedly one afternoon to say that he thought they needed some fresh air. He did not seem to mind that they were all living in the same room, but he did think they needed to be out of doors. He was dressed in his hospital whites, crisp and wrinkled at the same time, and

Lily thought he was flushed and excited. He was very tall, she thought.

"I have to go to the other side of the island," he said. "Why don't you come with me?"

They did not feel very energetic; in fact, they had not stirred at all in the last few days. Sheridan was right. They did need exercise and sunlight, but they did not feel like moving a muscle. They were too withdrawn and depressed.

"I'm going to Waianae," he said. "There's a friend of mine who's leaving home and needs some help."

Lily looked up at him. It was not like her father to be going all the way across the island to help someone move. He might do that for a new sculpture or a sixteenth-century Buddhist manuscript. Lily had never known him to have close friends. She was curious. He noticed her interest and said, "It's someone who has been treated unfairly."

Jack wandered over to him, and Sheridan ruffled the top of Jack's head. "Come on," he said energetically. Without interest or will, they listlessly followed him into the garden. "Where's Tōsi?" Lily asked, but no one bothered to answer.

Sheridan walked with both hands in his pockets across the springy, green lawn. He seemed jaunty and pleased with himself and it made Lily uneasy. Jack and Jessie had already acquiesced to his good spirits and were romping alongside him, refreshed by the sea wind and the sudden sense of space. Lily felt guilty.

When they reached the garage, Sheridan pushed a button at the sliding doors, and there was an oiled, smooth sound as a car pivoted on the turn-table inside, rotating so that it faced outward, ready for departure.

It was dark in the big, damp garage and it was only when they were inside the car that they saw someone sitting in the front seat. It was a girl. She was reading, lips moving silently, from a small, black book. She used her finger to keep her place under each word.

"You know Christmas," Sheridan said cheerfully, taking the car keys from a hook.

The girl smiled sweetly and nodded. She was very young, perhaps only seventeen. The car moved out into the light. Lily and Jessie and Jack settled uneasily in the back seat. Lily stared at the back of the girl's head. Sheridan turned through the gate onto the narrow main road. He drove quickly. The heavy overhanging trees made the way full of shadows. Lily saw that the girl's long black hair was thick and slightly oily. The windshield misted with humidity. Christmas delicately turned the pages of her book as if the tips of her fingers were dirty and Lily recognized the sound of tissue-paper pages. She was reading a prayer book. Jack and Jessie stared out the open windows. The black macadam steamed.

The other side of the island meant the country, the still-wild side of the island. Lily saw that the road Sheridan was taking led to the north shore, where they often went to fish by torchlight and where Earl had taught them to read the night sky for storms.

Sheridan left the main road for a bumpy dirt lane. A man was selling dried squid under a banana tree. "Oh, I want some," said Jessie, leaping to the window. Sheridan stopped. He argued happily with the old man over a few pennies and a bargain was made. Christmas laughed and turned back to Lily and quietly said something about prayers. Lily could not hear her. She saw yellow bruises on Christmas's soft, brown arm. Jessie passed around the squid, and Christmas handed Lily her Catholic missal. Lily noticed that she had no hair on her arms, that they were bruised but smooth. "It's a prayer about the Virgin," she finally heard Christmas say.

Lily leaned awkwardly over the seat to take the prayer

book. She saw her father squeeze Christmas's hand. Christmas smiled at Lily. She had little teeth, rounded at the edges.

Jessie carefully divided the last piece of squid. She was happy. Jack ate hungrily. Lily held Christmas's missal like a red-hot coal in her lap. She watched absently as the jungle quickly and without warning became the flat, pale green plateau where they grew pineapple. They passed the movie theater where she and her mother sometimes went on hot nights, carrying their own folding chairs on their heads. Christmas twisted around to ask what name she had chosen for her confirmation.

"Why don't you answer?" asked Sheridan. He smiled back at Lily in the mirror.

"Because I don't believe," Lily said.

"Don't be impolite," Sheridan said. He was still smiling. The dirt lane widened in the pineapple fields. It was becoming a road. The sea was on their right again.

Sheridan stopped the car before a corrugated-tin hut. They got out silently, stiff from the drive. The roof of the hut was overlaid with shiny new palm fronds. Christmas got out and looked back at Sheridan nervously. She sidled halfheartedly toward the hut. Lily saw that her father had not planned to go inside, but when Christmas hesitated, he walked around to the hut, bending low in the small, dark doorway, and nudged his children inside.

In the hut, in the dark, were an old Hawaiian woman and man. The man was sitting on the floor. They were as surprised to see Sheridan as he was to see them. Lily could tell that they were especially surprised to see children. She saw her father look quickly at Christmas with a moment's mistrust. Christmas did not seem to notice. Lily felt dizzy.

"Oh!" the old man said for no reason. He seemed angry, but the old woman handed them food on a ti leaf. Christmas made a funny whistling noise, as if she were ashamed of them. She was in a hurry. Jack began to eat nervously but when he noticed Lily and Jessie just staring, he put the food on the ground. Lily was too frightened to eat. Jessie felt for Lily's hand and squeezed it tightly.

"So you're the doctor," the old man said sarcastically.

"Why do you beat her?" Sheridan asked calmly.

"She is a bad girl, very bad girl."

Sheridan shook his head indulgently. Christmas hurriedly put some belongings into a paper bag. The children stood close against each other, not knowing why Christmas was a bad girl.

Lily realized that the old man was Christmas's father, the old woman was her mother.

Christmas laughed suddenly, brave because Sheridan was there, and said in a high, loud voice that she was going to live in town and never come back. Her father and mother lowered their heads. Jack put out a wet, sticky hand like a sleep-walker. The old man suddenly stood up. He was very fat. He began to shout and the mother hid her brown face in her apron. Sheridan said calmly that they were living in another century and that no one would tolerate their cruel ways. With Christmas laughing and sobbing gratefully on his arm, he pushed the children out of the hut.

The sun was just going down behind the mountains. They fell into the car, limp with confused sympathy for the poor, bad girl, and crossed the island in the dark to home. Jessie fell asleep on Lily's shoulder, and Jack held his face out into the warm, silky air. Lily just leaned her cheek against Jessie's head. Her hair smelled like the sea.

That night, Sheridan put the mistreated, gloating girl in the servant's quarters, with the distinction of a room of her own. Lily did not know what to think.

In the next days, she tried to stay out of Christmas's way, but one morning, very early, they nearly collided in the dark, wide hall. Christmas asked her whether she had learned the prayer to the Virgin for her confirmation. She smiled and stepped aside exaggeratedly to let Lily pass. It was such an unnecessary gesture that Lily looked back over her shoulder. No one was there. "Not yet," she said, "not yet," and she hurried away.

SIX

$\mathcal{T}$ōsɪ ᴀɴᴅ ʟɪᴛᴛʟᴇ Aɴɴᴀ were down at the far end of the beach. They were flying a kite. They had made it together the night before and they were both very proud of it, but I was not allowed to participate until they were sure that it would fly.

I was daydreaming in my chair near the water when the hotel manager stepped politely under my umbrella. I pretended to be asleep and watched him for several moments from beneath my eyelids while he searched anxiously for a surface on which to knock. Finally, he gave up and coughed. I opened my eyes.

"There is someone who wants to see you, madam," he said. He had been told when we first arrived that we desired privacy. We were very careful about making friends with other guests, having discovered years ago that it always ended in resentful disappointment for them and perplexed embarrassment for us. Tōsi's theory was that we did not turn out to be as exotic as we looked.

"Excuse me?"

"She insisted. What could I do, madam?"

I sat up, awkwardly tying the top of my suit, and looked around. To my astonishment, coming across the sand, in cowboy boots, was my sister, Jessie. She waved without smiling. Down by the white water, Tōsi and Anna were standing gloomily over the downed kite, as if it were a dead bird. The manager bowed slightly. I thought for a minute that he was going to click his heels in the soft sand but he merely walked off with a strange hitch, trying to shake the sand out of his pants cuffs. It was so like Jessie not to tell him who she was.

"Jessie," I said. My voice squeaked.

She was silhouetted against the sun and I had to squint to see her and shade my eyes. She stopped abruptly in front of me. I held up a towel to cover myself. She was so formidable. She was carrying a large satchel.

"Hi, sis," she said. She looked all around. She was elaborately casual. I stood up.

"How did you get here? Are you all right?"

"Credit card," she said. She smiled for the first time. "On a Bank of Maui card. For some reason, it takes four months to get the bill." I laughed.

"Why don't you take off your boots?" I said. I couldn't remember her ever wearing shoes. I regretted saying it. Jessie always accused me of trying to be her mother.

"Not all of us spend our lives wearing Bain de Soleil, you know."

"No," I said, ignoring her sarcasm. I was still so surprised to see her. It had been so long since Jessie and I were together. Perhaps it was because we were so young when we separated, and because we roamed so far apart, that our feelings for each other never seemed clear. We avoided each other. We avoided home. There was always the sense of danger, of feelings too volatile and tangled to allow us too much time together, and without our ever saying so, it seemed best for us to stay apart, to meet only in passing in the odd airport or hotel lobby.

When I left that first time, when Sheridan gave me, still a child, the ridiculous around-the-world airline ticket and I went to my grandmother's, they had patiently waited for me to return. But while they waited, I grew further and further away: as I thought about Sheridan's gift, I became convinced that he wanted me to stay away. Why else would he have so little guided me? Why else would he not have sent for me? I cashed in the return ticket and used that money while I looked for a job. I did not write to my father and he did not write to me.

Tōsi was still sent by Sheridan every year to Japan to study, and finally, when he had given up hope that I would ever return, he wrote to Sheridan to ask whether he might stay in Japan, and Sheridan had been pleased to give his permission. Tōsi was the only one who ever asked Sheridan whether he could leave.

Jessie just walked out one day. She stayed with people in houses on the road, a week or two in each one, working her way patiently down the road to the bus stop by the fishpond, where I used to wait in the spiky grass long before there even were other houses on the road to the Big House. The neighbors had been kind to her (she was only fifteen years old) and kinder still when it became obvious that Sheridan was not coming after her. With the help of her various hosts, she hoarded enough Blue Chip Stamps to turn them in for a one-way plane ticket to a neighboring island. She knew about a big ranch there, and the day she arrived she went to the foreman and talked herself into a job rubbing down and feeding the horses. She taught herself to ride and rope and brand. She learned quickly. She was accepted and encouraged by the old-timers. She must have been good, because they were very hard to please. She even won some local fame. She sent Tōsi the newspaper clippings from the *Kula Courier*. (He sent the same clippings to Jack in India, because months later I received from Jack a tattered Penguin paperback of psycho-analytic lectures about the obsession of some female adolescents for horses. Apparently this interest in horses was really a longing for the father's penis, or so the passages under-lined by Jack seemed to suggest.) She entered rodeos and won. She was several points shy of being a champion, but she was young and had years of competition ahead of her.

She looked older than I had pictured her. Her life in the outdoors. There was a tan line low on her forehead where she wore her hat. She looked uncomfortable in a blouse and skirt. I realized suddenly that I had thought of her as a cowgirl heroine riding through sage and maile, rounding up cows with sweetly melodic Hawaiian names. I stared at her. It wasn't romantic at all. It must have been very hard, physically hard and lonely, and isolated and peculiar.

"I've brought you something," she said. "I suppose that's why I'm here." She smiled and we sat down together on the chaise.

"I'm very happy to see you, Jessie, after so long. I just received your letter, and here you are. Here we are. It seems so strange that we're not children anymore."

"Haven't been for a long time," she said without emotion. She took off her boots.

"How are you?" I asked.

The question sounded odd, but she only laughed and said, "Swell. I was in Texas. In a rodeo. And also to buy some quarter horses for the ranch. I got one of those brochures at the airport and I looked up Grenadines and it didn't seem so far to come."

"Well, I'm happy you did."

She looked at me, trying to see whether I meant what I said. She was very skeptical. I turned so that she could look into my eyes and see that I did mean it. I knew she was uncomfortable. She had been that way all her life.

"The lawyers in San Francisco sent me this at Ulupalakua. They didn't know where you were. I thought I'd better give it to you myself. It's addressed to all of us, but somehow I felt it was meant for you." She pulled a big manila envelope from her bag and placed it heavily in my hands. Now it was my turn to look into her eyes for a clue to her real feelings. I felt that she was mocking and sarcastic.

"You needn't have gone to so much trouble."

"I wanted to. I wanted to see you. It's been almost two years." She was staring at the water. "Perhaps it's important," she said, looking at the envelope. Tōsi and Anna ran past, the kite a few yards behind them in the air. She smiled. "I wanted to see all of you." She stood up. "I was wondering where the little demon was. And is that Anna?" She seemed distracted and I thought she was only being polite. I thought she was suffering.

"How could you resist not opening it?" I asked. I held the heavy envelope in my hand as though weighing it.

"Easy," she said. She put her hand to her forehead. "I don't want anything to change the way I feel. I've worked hard to feel this way. It's taken a long time. I don't want it undone by sentiment. No more pilikia."

"How do you know what's inside? It may not be trouble, Jessie."

"It may not be. You know Father as well as I do. I'm not taking any chances."

"You hate him that much?" I was beginning to feel an uneasy awe.

"I'm glad he's disappeared. I hope he never comes back." She spoke casually, following Tōsi and Anna with her eyes as they trotted by, waving and shouting and pointing to the kite, which was now starting to climb in the sky. They were ecstatic. I waved back and smiled mechanically, hoping they would not stop, that I would have more time alone with her, but just as I thought they were off and away, Tōsi stopped short and stared. It took Anna some time to realize that he was no longer beside her and she stumbled, awkwardly trying to alter her course. Unknowingly, Tōsi had given life to the kite and it now flew high above us.

Jessie smiled when Tōsi reached us and they embraced. "How you doing?" she asked jokingly and he grinned and patted her on the shoulder. Her island accent had suddenly grown stronger. Jessie and Tōsi have always gotten along. I felt left out by their cheery good will. "Good going, Tōs," I said, pointing to the soaring kite. He had forgotten all about it in his excitement and was surprised to see it flying so high. Anna crashed messily into my lap, wet and sandy on top of the manila envelope. She was out of breath. "Look who's here!" I said, drumming up excitement. She was more interested in the kite.

"Did you miss your auntie?" Jessie asked. Anna looked at me, then looked at Jessie and nodded. "Well, maybe," Jessie said and laughed. We all laughed and Tōsi pulled Anna up by the hand. He pretended to be dragged off by the kite. He knew that Jessie's appearance meant something important. He was giving us time alone. "I'll see you later," he shouted into the wind.

Jessie fastened the latches of the satchel. "You look like a courier," I said.

"I feel like one," she said. She stretched restlessly. I picked up her heavy boots and without speaking we left the beach. At the top of the cliff, we did not stop at the bar but turned silently down the narrow walk that wound through the hotel grounds. Every few yards, nailed to a tree trunk or stuck in the ground before a bush, was a tiny sign identifying the genus: *Magnifera Indica, Ficus Benghalensis, Delonix Regia.* We walked Indian file, I in front with the boots and the envelope, Jessie behind with her satchel. We had walked this way, barefoot on wet, sandy stones, under the aromatic branches of Moreton figs, many, many times. We went as far as we could go, until the path ended at the low building where the hotel laundry was done. We could hear loud laughter and arguing as we came near but it stopped suddenly when a woman in a pink uniform saw us from a window. I felt happy. As we turned around, Jessie leading now, I saw a slight smile on her face too.

At the bungalow, I sentimentally made jasmine tea while she walked up and down the terrace. I set the table quickly and put some guavas and biscuits on a pretty plate and called her to the table.

She drank some tea. If she noticed that it was jasmine, she did not say. I was the one who was nostalgic. That was why she had come so far to give me the big envelope. I wondered whether she was still so ill at ease. She must have been, because often she could not open her eyes when she spoke to me. She was unaware of it, but she would throw her head back and peer down at me, her eyelids fluttering in an endless blink. She confuses me with Anna, even now.

"How could you have gotten in touch with Father?" she asked suddenly.

"Not this again. Please, Jessie. Have a cookie and shut up."

"How could you have spoken to him?"

"Three times in ten years. Once in the VIP lounge at the Los Angeles airport. Once on the telephone. Once on a radio, ship to shore." She knew all this.

She lit a cigarette and flung the burned match into a teacup. "Don't you understand that to recognize him is to validate him? To support him? Revisionist reality."

"I thought he should know he had a grandchild. He's an old man. He's not important in the old way anymore. I've recovered from him. It took a long time, but I have."

"I can never forgive him. I want him out of my life," she said furiously.

"He *is* out of your life. He has *no* interest in you. Not the slightest. That's what makes you so angry. That's why you're afraid to open the goddamn envelope. You suspect he cares about me, but I promise you, he has no interest in *any* of us!"

She picked up the teapot and held the lid down with the hand holding the cigarette. She poured herself tea. Her hands were trembling. Bits of jasmine petals from the bottom of the pot swirled in the cup. She lifted the cup to her mouth but did not drink, and put it down again. Her little finger stuck out when she held the cup.

"Vronsky wanted to leave Anna Karenina for holding a cup like that," I said illogically. She made me very nervous. "At the end, when she was desperate and difficult."

"You identify too much with fictional characters. That's always been *one* of your problems." She lifted the cup again and drank, little finger out stiff.

"Why don't you just forgive him and get it over with?" I asked.

"That's easy for you to say."

"No, it's not. Nothing is easy where they're concerned. You think my life has been a normal one?"

"I hate him."

"You're furious all over again because he's disappeared. He may be dead and you've not yet managed to get your revenge. He may be out of your reach now, Jessie. When I spoke to him the last time, I was shocked. His voice was old and watery."

"I know what he sounds like," she said. She stood up and went to the edge of the terrace, where the bougainvillea began. "We are completely different." She pulled leaves off a bush.

"We are?"

"You've always been with Tōsi." She spun around to face me. She did not blink now. She folded her arms tightly across her chest, tucking her hands into her armpits. I suddenly thought that she might hurt me, that she was dangerous. She came across the terrace and needlessly began to stack the unused plates. A knife rolled off and fell to the ground noisily.

"This whole relationship has got to be restructured," she said firmly.

"What relationship?"

"Our relationship. That's another reason I'm not staying here."

"Oh," I said, and bent over to pick up the knife. She stood over me. "You're not staying?" She made me feel helpless.

"And I'm not going to try to find him. I refuse. He sucks you into his madness. You fall for it."

"I do?"

"I do. Tōsi does. We all do. Revisionist reality." She rubbed her forehead. "God!" she said loudly. "Where's the envelope?" She looked around wildly.

I went to her and put my arm around her. "I put it in the sitting room. It's all right."

She didn't like me to touch her. As a way of escaping, she turned my wrist over to look at my watch. "I'm at another hotel," she said. "I'm only staying the night." She rubbed her forehead again.

"You are?"

She picked up the clumsy-looking satchel. She did see herself as a courier. I felt very sad. I wanted to hold her. I wanted her to hold me.

"Earth to Mars, Earth to Mars, do you read me?" she asked. She made me laugh. I have always thought Jessie was very funny.

"Over and out," she said and was gone.

❧

Later, when Tōsi and Anna trudged home exhausted from the beach, Tōsi was surprised that she was staying at another hotel.

"And she doesn't want to see us tonight," I said.

He came out to where I was sitting alone on the terrace. He looked suspiciously as if he was going to say something serious and I clapped my hands over both ears. He frowned but said nothing and went back into the bungalow. I was not ready for his sensible impartiality. I was afraid he would make me feel guilty and jealous by taking her side. Tōsi was still my conscience.

He brought out a fresh pot of tea, but he did not look at me, and when he started to leave, I invited him to sit down. I have asked him many times not to wait on me, his role of servant long over, but he insists that these small attendances give him pleasure and I believe him. Now, in turn, I poured a cup for him as delicately as I could and he smiled, our kinship restored.

"She brought us papers from the lawyer," I said. "About Father. About Anna. About all of us, I imagine. She didn't want them. She doesn't even want to know what's inside." He looked at me curiously. "Perhaps she's smart. She hasn't arranged her life riding horses around the rim of a volcano to have it changed now." We smiled into our teacups. The cup warmed my hands.

"I suppose," he said quietly, "there's something that I should tell you now."

I did not feel dread, exactly, but a sudden tiredness. "Really?" He nodded. "Right now?" He nodded again and smiled.

"It's not bad. I've wanted to tell you for some time," he said. "About twenty years." He seemed happy and even giddy. I rested my head on the back of my chair and closed my eyes.

"Okay," I said.

He spoke quickly. "When I used to go home, although I can't say it really was home, when your father would send me to Japan, did you know where I really went? You thought Kyoto to study religion and art, but I stopped there only at the beginning and end of each trip."

"You always brought me beautiful presents."

"I would go to Hiroshima," he said.

I waited for him to continue but he was waiting for me to remember. It made me nervous. I felt his excitement while I tried to fit together all my small bits of knowledge, pieces of conversation overheard, canceled stamps, birth dates and whispers. I was not sure that I understood. It was an effort for him to be patient.

"Is that why your eyes were always light-sensitive?" I asked stupidly. He nodded. He pitied my confusion and hurried on.

"He found me there with my mother after the bomb was

89

dropped. She was wearing a flowered summer kimono when the bomb fell, and the heat and flash made a pattern of the flowers on her naked body. She was dead but she had gone into labor. He was there. I was born into his hands. He kept me."

For Tōsi, it was simple, but I was full of wonder. "You had no other family? They were dead?" I felt ashamed of the Americans and the bomb, and I felt something worse. I was envious of his bond with my father. I turned my face away from him. My first emotion had been envy, not sorrow for his mother's death or his suffering or the suffering of his people.

"I had cousins surviving, the ones I would visit each year, but he didn't care. He brought me to your mother, to Anna. She was eight months pregnant with you." I didn't speak. "He is quite a ruthless man. You know that about him."

"And what do you think?" I finally looked at him. "What do you think about this?"

"It is too late now to think one way or the other. I loved him. And Anna-san."

"He stole you."

"Yes."

"When did you find out?"

"The first time he sent me back. When we were eight."

"Then you really are my brother, in a way." I started to laugh. "Wait until Jack hears. He always said you were." Tōsi smiled. I jumped up and walked up and down the terrace. I felt elated.

"Is that why you were so strange when you came back the first time? You broke my heart."

"I was oppressed with gratitude. I felt that I could never repay him. Very Japanese of me."

"But why was he there?" I asked, stopping suddenly.

"Studying."

"He was always studying."

"The government sent him right after the bomb to study the effects. He was a radiologist. It was a secret. They were proud of his work. His hair went white."

"How do you know?"

"The cousins. Sheridan-san was famous."

"Jack found a picture of him once and I didn't believe it was Father." Tōsi shrugged and smiled again. "Well," I said, "I am very sorry."

He understood what I meant. Not sorry that Sheridan-san had kept him.

"I think we should look for him," he said.

"Okay."

"I've already begun."

"With the cousins?" I laughed. "You didn't waste any time."

"He's not there. Not in Japan at all. They checked carefully. They would do anything for him."

"But he's alive?" I felt an ache in my jaw as I tried not to cry.

"I don't know."

"The envelope!" I shouted. We had forgotten all about it. I ran to the sitting room and brought the envelope back to the terrace. It seemed even bigger and more unwieldly than before.

"You open it." I put it in his hands, but he gave it back to me and I unraveled the brown string in the back and pulled out the papers. It had not been opened for years. There were stock certificates and oil-well leases and Father's honorable discharge papers from the army and birth certificates for all of us, except Tōsi, and his will. There was also a small sealed envelope addressed in his hand "To my wife, Anna, to open upon my death."

"This means they think he's dead," I said. I glanced briefly at the will, which left the estate in equal parts to my mother, myself, Jack, Jessie and Tōsi. Tōsi picked up the letter to Anna in both hands and stared at the writing. He turned it over and over. He reminded me of a magician trying to guess the contents of a letter sent up by someone in the audience.

"Jessie needn't have left so quickly," he said.

"She was afraid." I shook out the envelope. There were a few more pieces of paper, honorary degrees from two universities, and a note from the San Francisco lawyers, explaining that they had held the envelope as instructed for six months after Sheridan Shields's disappearance, that they were forwarding it on, including a bill for two thousand dollars for the work they had done. There was nothing in the envelope about Hiroshima.

"You needn't have told me," I said. "I hope you're not sorry."

"I never understood why it was a secret. Perhaps he was afraid it would mark me. Not for myself, but for others. Most Americans thought the bomb was good. They were told the war would continue if they didn't drop it."

"Would it have?"

"No." He was matter-of-fact. "They just wanted to test their bomb."

"I don't think Father is dead," I said. I surprised myself.

Inside the bungalow Anna woke from her nap and called out. We both got up, but Tōsi had a head start. He loves her when she just wakes up, all damp and rosy and happy to see you. I could hear the change in her voice from longing to pleasure as she caught sight of him through the open window.

SEVEN

WITH THE EXCEPTION of Lily, Jack and Jessie, the Big House absorbed Christmas without too much trouble. Even Tōsi seemed to accommodate her, an impartiality that made Lily furious. It also confused her. It indicated a generosity that Lily was unable to give. Lily held on to the idea that adults were accountable for their actions. Tōsi seemed to have learned from her father the unacceptable notion that, in the end, it did not much matter what people did: not only did it not much matter, it did not matter one way or the other. Only the small details, like politeness, mattered.

So Lily was not on particularly good terms with Tōsi. She avoided him and perhaps he avoided her. She spent most of her time with Jack. Together they rode their salt-encrusted bikes to Tigger's rented house, having tried several times to reach her by telephone, and the gardener told them she had gone away. Two, maybe three weeks, he said.

School started, but only Lily and Jessie were sent off early each morning in the dark. Jack, after the first day, had refused to go back to school. Lily admired him for it and regretted that she had not thought of it first. It was not that she did not like school, but staying at home would have kept her closer to Anna, or Anna's ghost, now that Anna was gone.

No one could persuade Jack to change his mind. Sheridan talked to him sensibly, the maids teased him, and Tōsi tried to bribe him, but he would have none of it. Everyone secretly respected him; he was so firm and dignified.

While the girls went off quietly each morning at six, he got up and dressed himself, the sky still chill and dark, and wandered about the still-sleeping house like an old man prematurely retired, examining his prize-winning orchids, tending the pigeons, straightening and restraightening his shelves. No one bothered him after it became clear that he would not change his mind. Christmas, if she came home for lunch from the hospital, tried to make conversation with him in the kitchen, but he would have nothing to do with her.

They never knew why he would not go back to school. Perhaps the first day another child had repeated some gossip about Anna. He would never tell them. Sheridan brought books home for him, and Tōsi took him into the garden to pick fruit and vegetables. Lily suspected that Tōsi may have been a little rough on him because Tōsi had always wanted to go to the proper school in town, but Jack never complained.

Unlike her brother, Jessie never stopped talking, at least to Lily. Jessie suspected that Lily knew more about their mother's disappearance than she said. As Jessie became more insistent and frantic, Lily grew more withdrawn and despondent. She tried to convince Jessie that she was not hiding anything, and she wasn't, but Jessie simply could not believe that there was no explanation of Anna's abandonment. For Jessie, Christmas became the embodiment of whatever it was that had gone wrong, and although the household could not explain why

94

Christmas was living in the house, since Sheridan did not pay her any particular or conspicuous attention, in her heart Jessie blamed the plump, eager-to-please girl. Jessie actually hissed at Christmas whenever she saw her.

As for Sheridan, he seemed unperturbed. He was unchanged. Full of his usual refined enthusiasms, he was teaching the boat boys how to fly-fish. They had never even seen a fly rod or reel before. He had already spent some time training Earl, who was reluctant to change his ways at first, having been at the Aala market one afternoon in December 1936 when a Japanese boat brought in a black marlin, taken off Waianae, that weighed 1540 pounds. At that time, it was the biggest marlin taken by any method. Lily had patiently heard the story many times from Earl. He was understandably disturbed by Sheridan's odd, new way of fishing.

Not that Sheridan wasn't good. He had begun when he was a boy, working the clear, narrow chalk streams of southern Pennsylvania. The islands had no trout streams, so he simply took to the Pacific Ocean. To adjust his cast, he practiced on the lawn, casting to small banana leaves placed at intervals of fifteen and twenty and thirty yards. He cast over and over again, until to his satisfaction the exquisite and colorful handmade fly landed accurately at the mouth-end of each leaf.

The local fishermen thought Sheridan was crazy, and imitated him behind his back, waving their arms wildly over their heads and giggling. Earl was teased, but he minded less after Sheridan's last fight with a huge striped marlin. It was brought to the side after four hours, shook loose three gaffs and fought five more hours before being boated.

Sheridan never fished without a loaded revolver. During some months of the year, when the sharks were on the rampage, it was almost impossible to boat a fish that did not have huge, jagged bites taken out of it. Sometimes only a bony jaw hung at the end of the line. It was a terrifying thing to see, a crazed shark, sometimes two or three, making blind-eyed passes at the hooked fish, thrashing and bloodied. When there was a shark nearby, Earl automatically gave the hooked fish its head, hoping it could twist free. A fresh fish had a chance of outrunning the shark, but a tired fish was lost. Sheridan fired at the sharks, but rarely killed one. Once, though, he severed the line with a bullet through the water. He said he could not have hit the line in a million years if he had tried.

But Sheridan's obsession was the dolphin fish, the mahimahi. Lily had seen her father catch barracuda and marlin and bonefish on a fly, but never a mahimahi, which has more speed than any other gamefish. She knew that he dreamed about dolphin.

One morning, Jessie and Lily were allowed to accompany him. Jessie was late getting up, so only Lily went out with Earl at sunrise to catch the flying fish needed for bait. The mahimahi were out, too, feeding, cruising fast just beneath the surface, behind the flying fish, waiting the four or five seconds between skips until their breakfast bounced back into the water. The flying fish made a strange, squeaking sound, wings chafing and whirring. When they came in, Sheridan and Jessie were waiting at the dock.

Earl was excited and the boat boys were shy and anxious. Jessie was allowed to sit up in the tower with Earl. In keeping with Sheridan's custom, no one spoke. Lily could see the soles of Jessie's bare feet.

The outrigger towers were rigged with heavy lines, drag-ging the bait. Each line was doubled back and held with a clothespin. When the mahimahi went for the bait, the pin would snap loose and the line fall back slack for only an in-stant before Earl threw the throttle forward and the line snapped taut and the hook was set. Lily knew this was called a teaser. Because mahimahi travel in pairs, mates feeding together, the companion fish always comes to the aid of the hooked fish. And it was the companion fish, the rescuer, that Sheridan was trying to trick into taking a fly.

The lines set, the boys waited. Earl drove in big circles, looking for flying fish or the serrated lines on the surface that meant activity below. It was still early. The sun was only a few inches above the horizon. Sheridan stood the whole time, rod in his right hand, leader in his left, watching for movement. They trolled for an hour. Then, as it always happened, quickly and unexpectedly no matter how long you had been waiting, the clothespin snapped free, the line fell slack, and they rocked on their feet as the boat lurched forward. The line jerked once as the hook was set, then streamed out as the fish tried to escape.

It was not certain that a mahimahi had been hooked. It could have been an ahi or the great ulua, but Earl didn't think so: it didn't run like an ulua, not quite as heavy. The boat boy and Lily stood at the side, staring into the wake as the line was reeled in and the hooked fish was pulled closer to the boat. Then they saw it. It was a mahimahi. Lily was suprised at its color, iridescent jade and gold, spotted with turquoise, and purple like an iris. It was very beautiful, thrashing and twisting twenty-five feet off the side, trying to shake free, charging the boat, then darting away. Lily had only seen one in the kitchen, gray and blunt-headed and dead. She did not know it looked like a rainbow. She said so to her father and he nodded, preoccupied and concentrating, and asked hadn't she read Byron?

Lily looked off the back and saw, coming up from the depths, the mate. She did not call out. No one else had seen it. Earl idled the boat. The hooked fish was tired and held in perfect position. Lily wondered nervously whether fish could talk, whether they had a way of warning each other. Still she did not point to it. She wanted to stamp her feet and frighten it away. It disappeared. They waited patiently. Lily began to relax, but then it came out suddenly from under the boat, frantic and angry, and Earl, with his sharp eyes, saw it at once and stood up and pointed.

The boy and Lily retreated to the bow, as they had been taught, out of the way of the whipping line, and Sheridan cast to the wild fish. It did not take it. It knew, Lily hoped, that it was a trick. The idea was that in its greed, or perhaps the instinct to take food when it was there in front of it even if it was not hungry, or in confusion about its mate, the fish would take the fly.

Sheridan cast again. Lily thought that it was lovely to watch him. This time, easily and greedily, the wild fish took the fly. Sheridan jerked the rod to set the hook. The reel spun and shrieked as the fish ran out the line. There was the danger that the two lines would become entangled, so a boy jumped forward and pulled in the tired, hooked fish. "It is a female," he said quietly to Lily. Earl shouted orders. As Sheridan tentatively began to wind in the male fish, it took off again and water sprayed off the reel. The first fish was pulled safely to the side, where with one quick and deft movement, the boy gaffed it with a loud thud and heaved it up over the side. The fish gasped and worked its gills, then quickly and as though by magic, the blue and gold washed in ripples of color, runs of light, off its body, ripples of gold streaming off the fish, leaving it steely gray and dead. It was a different fish. Lily stared at the deck to see whether it left a rainbow puddle beneath it, but the water that washed under the boards was bloody sea water.

Sheridan had reeled in the second fish, but tired as it must have been, it fought hard whenever it got near the boat. Perhaps it could see the boy crouched on the rear platform, gaff in hand. At last it darted near enough, and the boy, inexperienced, not realizing that the tippet was delicate and light, grabbed the tippet with one hand, preparing to gaff with the other. In the same instant Sheridan shouted "No!" and the tippet snapped and the fish was free.

They all looked at Sheridan. It wasn't the boy's fault. Sheridan knew that. Without speaking, he slowly began to wind in the line, the reel clicking and spraying water as he guided it between his two fingers. The fish had taken the line out almost to the backing. Earl waited, one arm around the wheel, twisted sideways on the seat, looking back over his shoulder. Jessie had not moved the whole time. Finally Sheridan said, "It's all right," still working on the reel, and the boy wiped his eyes with his fishy fists and Earl turned back to the wheel and swung the boat around for home.

Lily wondered whether the male fish would be able to work free the big hook. She was embarrassed to ask. They ate the female for lunch and she felt surprised and guilty that it tasted so good.

❧

Along the side of the house that faced the orchard, there was a gallery fifty feet long. It had a parquet floor with the seal of the territory laid out in the center in different kinds of native wood. The outer wall of the gallery and the two ends were screened from floor to roof, and the inside wall had a dado of koa wood and then glass to the ceiling. The gallery was built high enough above the ground so that it resembled a barge floating in a lake of plumeria and shower trees. The trees were encouraged to grow high around it. Anna had never permitted furniture in the gallery. Only a wooden fan hung from the ceiling and it had not worked since Lily was a baby. Very old, tall, red and yellow feather standards once used by the great kings leaned in each cool corner.

The children were allowed to take their mats into the gallery to sleep on very hot nights, and twice a year Anna gave a big afternoon party there. Once a friend of Tigger's must have really thought she was floating above the trees. There was a trade wind that ruffled all the leaves like little green waves at her knees and the blossoms like tiny fish slipping in and out of the waves. She became sick and had to be carried away.

On the days of the parties, Tōsi and Jack and Lily sat in the lowest branches of the trees. They were invisible from the gallery above. Toward sunset, musicians noiselessly slipped into the orchard and played sad old island songs beneath them. The children were suspended between the soft, tinny slides of the steel guitars and the sound of polite laughter and ice in glasses.

That fall, because their mother had gone away, there was no party. Instead, Christmas used the gallery to practice the hula. She took the old phonograph from the playroom and placed it on top of the territorial seal, using three extension cords to connect it to a wall socket in the dark sitting room on the other side of the glass. The sitting room was Anna's room. Anna used to sit at her desk every morning and write a letter to her mother in Philadelphia. She never missed a day.

Since she had gone, the room had been unused. Lily would sneak in there to sit in Anna's chair and study the things she had left behind, trying to solve the mystery of her going. She could not understand it. Her father still had said nothing to her. Tōsi could not find out where she was, and even Tigger had nothing to say. Lily had quizzed her when she returned, but Tigger told her only what she already knew. Lily reasoned that her mother must not have intended staying away long, because nothing had been removed or put away. On her desk were an open pack of Camel cigarettes, her gray stationery, three Estabrook fountain pens and a dried bunch of crown-flowers, tied with raffia, that Jack had given her. In the top drawer of her desk were a Japanese-English dictionary and a yellowed certificate citing her father for "Bravery Beyond the Call of Duty" as an ambulance driver, dated 1916.

Her appointment diary was open. She had written in her three weekly appointments with her doctor and she had written them for months in advance. This was the doctor she went to see in a taxi. It was very unusual to see a taxi in the country but it came three afternoons a week, at the same time, to pick her up. It returned her precisely two hours later. She refused to drive herself after she had two minor accidents in the first week of her sessions.

Slipped inside the back pages of the diary Lily found a yellowed photograph cut from a magazine. It was old and its edges were frayed. The picture was of a big white house with green shutters and columns in the front. The caption read "Old Oaks, the fabulous Main Line estate of Millicent Wagner photographed especially for *Town and Country*." It meant nothing to Lily. She did not think Mrs. Wagner's house was as pretty as the Big House. She wondered why her mother had saved the picture.

Sitting at the desk, in the dim, still light, studying the photograph, she heard the song "Beyond the Reef" coming from the gallery. It was her mother's favorite song. She turned around and through the glass she could see Christmas, in shorts and a halter top, dancing in her bare feet. The record was scratched and she bent down to start it again. Lily watched for a long time. Christmas could not see her because Lily was in the dark. Sitting there at the big desk in the cool room watching her, Lily felt very superior. Christmas was impatient. She had no concentration and the scratched record made her irritable. When she stamped her little foot, the needle jumped on the record. Lily slipped out to find Tōsi.

He was in his room at the back of the house, cutting out the words to songs from a *Hit Parade* magazine and pasting each clipping into a big scrapbook. He could not read English perfectly yet but he saved the clippings, he once told Lily, in anticipation of the day when he could. It seemed silly because he could sing all the songs in English already, but Lily knew it would be unwise to point this out. The scrapbook was very thick.

"She's dancing in the gallery!" Lily said. Tōsi shrugged and kept on cutting. " 'Cherry Pink and Apple Blossom White,' " he said, not looking up.

"She's out there doing the hula!"

"Cha-cha-cha," he said.

"Are you trying to be funny?"

He stopped and looked up, but didn't close the scissors.

"Practice. She practices all the time now. She needs to." He went back to work, ignoring Lily.

Lily soon discovered that she did practice all the time, starting and restarting the scratched record. Everywhere Lily went in the house, maids and cooks and gardeners hummed the music. No one seemed to know exactly why she was dancing in the gallery. Lily began to hate the song, which slowly took over the house, and she no longer went to sit at her mother's desk. Lily wandered like a lost soul.

⌒ℨ

One afternoon at tea, Sheridan came into the playroom. Jessie and Jack and Lily were sitting at the big table watching the only station they could get on television, an American station, and eating rice balls and ice cream. Since Anna had gone no one was much in charge, at least not in the kitchen, and they ordered whatever they were in the mood to eat. Sheridan didn't notice. He wouldn't have minded if he did notice.

He turned off the television and told the maid to have them ready to go out in half an hour. This made them very excited. Even the maid was filled with a sense of joyful preparation because they all thought it must have something to do with Anna. They dressed very quickly. Tōsi came in already dressed. He had slicked down his hair with pomade.

It was drizzling when they got into the car. They drove a very long way. Sheridan was quiet and no one else spoke. The rain stopped and started again.

They finally came to a field on the far side of a fishing village, where a small canvas tent had been set up. There were strings of white lights and inside the tent a wooden stage had been erected and a five-man band was seated in folding chairs on the edge of the platform. There was an announcer in a sky-blue tuxedo and red carnation leis. The children, except for Tōsi, were very sleepy. The warm, light rain was visible in the light from the small bulbs swinging over the black field. It was crowded and difficult to see the stage. The tent did not extend very far beyond the stage and the rain fell on them.

After waiting a long time, being afraid to move and lose their places, they saw pretty girls in long, pastel tulle gowns come onto the stage one by one. They sang or danced or recited poetry in front of a microphone. It was hard to hear them and once the microphone broke. A girl in a pink dress that stood straight out from her waist played the harp, and her dress kept getting caught in the strings. Lily noticed that Sheridan was smiling, even though they could not see or hear very well and Jessie was getting irritable. Tōsi stared at the stage, enraptured. Finally, Lily heard the announcer say, "Christmas Valdemos, our last contestant this evening, dancing for you the haunting 'Beyond the Reef.'"

Sheridan clapped loudly and lifted Jessie onto his shoulders so that she could see better. The crowd, wet now and weary, clapped because she was the last one and it would soon be over. Christmas smiled coyly and nodded her head and the little orchestra began to play and she danced the hula that Lily had watched her practice in the gallery. Lily looked at Tōsi but he was watching Christmas in a trance. She was wearing a pikake lei and green velvet holoku to match her beautiful eyes. Sheridan clapped again. Lily could not get Tōsi to look at her.

Early the next morning Tōsi tiptoed into Lily's room. She was awake. "She didn't win," he said, giggling. "She needs more practice." He put his hand over his mouth to stop the sound and padded out. He laughed all the way down the hall.

They put the Japanese lanterns up, stringing them through the shower trees. With the thick pink and yellow blossoms, the lanterns would be hidden until the sun fell and they were lit.

Lily had felt the excitement all day. Even Tōsi missed his lesson and had been put to work cleaning out the lily pond. At first, in the morning, Lily thought it might be about her mother. Tōsi said no. Lily hadn't asked him; he just looked at her face and said "No." "How do you know?" she asked. He just turned away and lifted a koi out of the pond with his net. Lily wanted to hurt him or push him into the pond. She grabbed the end of the net pole and yanked it, and the red, fat fish flipped out of the net onto the brick path. The fish lay stunned, tail arched, gills gaping, then suddenly it went flat and still. Tōsi gently picked it up, and, holding it by the tail, submerged it in the cool water and moved it back and forth, trying to force the gills open and shut by the surge and pull of the water. Lily walked back to the Big House, pleased with herself and singing. From the cane road, she could already hear them shaking out the lauhala mats.

Her father was giving a party. That was why the lanterns were tied in the trees. The younger children would be dressed, although no one would see them, and her good dress had already been laid out on her bed. Her mother liked parties, she thought. Lily wondered if she really would be there: of course she would be there. Why else would Father be having a party? Her mother had a dress from China made of gold that she often wore to parties. Perhaps she would wear that. Lily knew it was still in her closet, because she went into Anna's room every few days to look at her things. There was also the black ribbon dress, Lily thought excitedly. I would recommend that for a hot night like tonight. She may even let me watch her dress, all sliding and sinewy, the sound of silk eased up stockinged legs, shoetrees snapped out of satin shoes, heavy Chinese scent and rustle. I'll have to stand on the dressing-table stool to fasten the hooks she cannot reach and she will hold up her hair in back with her thin, brown arm so that I can lock the clasp of her necklace. The back of her neck will be damp, the black hair stained and curling. She will ask me, "What do you think?" It is just a game because we both know what I think, that she is wonderful.

Lily realized she had better get dressed quickly herself if she was going to have time to help her mother.

Tōsi came into her room without knocking. "What's the matter with you?" she asked him. He just stared, as usual.

"I have to hurry," she said.

"It's too late."

She looked at the clock on the bureau. "Tōsi," she said, shaking her head impatiently. He stood there stubbornly, his hands behind his back. She finished dressing, even though he remained there. "Go away," she said.

He dropped the red fish at her feet. Its mouth was open. It had not yet begun to smell, which surprised Lily. It looked alive. Its color was less bright, that was all. When she looked up, Tōsi was gone. She took her party shoes out of their box and put the fish in and put the top back on. She really hadn't much time. Her mother had certainly dressed herself by now.

Hair patted down with water, no time for flowers, she hurried down the long hall to the reception room. To her dismay, she could hear that guests had already arrived. The big koa doors opening onto the verandah were thrown back and two maids waited there. One of them, Malia, had forgotten to put on slippers.

Lily noticed that she could not hear her own footsteps as she came down the hall and stepped eagerly into the bright, big room. It was filled with people. No one took any notice of her. She looked for her mother. She looked for people that she knew. It seemed strange that no one paid her the slightest attention because she suddenly felt very large and conspicuous, as though her body were growing. Her body *was* growing. Stretching and climbing, she grew up and up. Soon she would reach the ceiling, maybe even crash through the roof into the night sky, like the boys in the Wet Cave. She was sure she saw her mother in the far corner of the room. She was wearing a white ginger lei. Even though she was gigantic and afraid of stepping on her father's guests and hurting them, she tried to push her way gently through the crowd to her.

Then she saw her father. He was sitting on a sofa. He looked very handsome, and although small, he looked happy. Christmas was sitting beside him, like a doll. Lily felt the top

of her head, still wet, brush against the chandelier. It made
a soft tinkling sound not unlike the tinkling sound of laughter
coming from below.

Each time Lily woke, there was a different face in front of
her: the white face would be suspended above the light summer blanket, and the face usually belonged to Jessie. She and
Tōsi took turns sitting on the low chair at the end of the bed.
Jessie had a particular affection for Lily when she was ill.
Jack was frightened, but Jessie seemed to enjoy it as she
waited, still and silent, a small, round, unattached face. She
sat there for hours. Every time Lily opened her eyes she was
there.

Jessie liked the delirium. "What was that?" she would ask,
very casually, fearful of startling Lily and breaking the spell.
It was as though she hoped to receive a special message: for
all of her short life, Jessie had been convinced that Lily knew
something that no one else knew. She believed the proof of
this was the special love Anna had always had for Lily. She
was waiting for the key to break the code. She wanted to
know how to get that love.

When Tōsi came to relieve her, she was reluctant to go. She
anxiously made him promise to give back her seat the moment
she returned. She also made him promise to remember everything Lily said while she was away. Tōsi had to agree to all
of this before she would give up the chair, before she would
even turn her head away, talking out of the side of her mouth
like a bad ventriloquist, afraid to displace even the air around
her.

With a small sigh, breath escaping from her at last, she got
up stiffly, her face suddenly a part of her small, plump body.
She left the room backward. Lily thought she was a ghost.

107

Tōsi sat down noisily in her place, sniffed once or twice and began to study his lessons. Lily, safe with Tōsi, could finally close her eyes and sleep.

She had decided not to get up until her mother returned. If Anna was dead, she would never get up. Lily listened to the loud click and hum of the garden sprinklers as the water began its arc outside her window, over the jasmine. A few drops thudded against the French doors before the fan of water arched and fell back over the flowers. She listened as it began again its unhurried climb. She listened to the men patiently and slowly sweeping the driveway with palm branches all the hot afternoon. She knew when they had reached the banyan tree because the mynah birds shrieked and scolded. The men paid no attention. This happened every day.

One morning Tōsi came earlier than usual to relieve Jessie. She didn't want to leave, feeling the morning to be an especially fruitful time for delirium, but he was very insistent and swore to memorize everything that happened in her absence. She slid away, a floating balloon face, and he sat on the bed and handed Lily a mango.

"You must get up now," he said. She ate the mango slowly. "Come with me," he said. "I know about Anna."

Lily listened to the men clipping vines outside. She wrapped the mango seed in a piece of Kleenex and put it on the bedside table, careful not to knock over the water jug. Every movement seemed to require Lily's full concentration.

Tōsi went to the closet door and opened it. There was a terrible smell from the fish in the shoebox. Lily got out of bed and he took down the box with the dead fish and she followed him out.

Behind the house, beyond the kitchen garden that Anna used to tend like an English lady, beyond the orchid greenhouse and the fruit orchards and the thick and wild, shiny-leaved gardenias, there began the kiawe forest. It was not a fairy-tale forest, but a wood that was found only in hot climates. Lily had seen pictures of the same forest in Mexico, although it was called by another name.

The kiawe trees were squat and wiry and rugged. There were no bowers. You could not picnic in this forest. You could not even sit under a tree. It was thorned scrub, scratchy and dry, and it made good fire kindling, fast-burning and aromatic. No birds or animals lived in the kiawe forest. At first glance, the trees did not even appear leaved, but they were, gray-green chips of leaves on jagged barbed-wire branches. The trees were not tall, not so high that you could not see over them. And above and beyond, there was nothing but cloudless sky and the velvet-green haze of the rain forests in the foothills. Lily thought it was like being in the dirty bottom of an empty blue and green cup.

Tōsi and Lily often went into the kiawe to look for bombs. During the war with Japan, American soldiers had lived in the forest and they left behind canteens and helmets and bayonets and bombs. The bombs looked like bombs: there was never any mistaking one, although they were rusty and mildewed at the same time. Fan said the Marines had not lived there: they came and stayed only two nights in 1943, leaving the bombs and ration cans behind in their haste to get away. The kiawe was worse than the Japanese they expected any minute to overrun the island like slant-eyed mice. Fan was very scornful of the Marines. She lived in the kiawe forest.

We must be going to see her, Lily thought, because Tōsi is in the middle of the wood and I am right behind him. Fan did not like visitors. She had left the kiawe only once, they said, when, after the Japanese air attack, she waded into the surf to put lighted cigarettes between the bloody lips of dying American boys. She also stripped the ones already dead of their helmets, which she used to tile the roof of her house. The girls in the Big House were afraid of her. She was Chinese.

She lived in a small, one-room shack with her thin, long-legged dogs and a tame mongoose. Lily did not know how she lived, although sometimes she had seen the skin of a wild boar stretched over poles to dry and fish bones on the dusty path, so she must have been given food, perhaps in exchange for spells and wishes. Lily knew her father sent Fan money, because she had seen him give it to Tōsi.

Tōsi did not speak and she did not speak, so intent were they on avoiding the thorns and snags of the kiawe. They could hear the bark of Fan's dogs as they got nearer. The shack always appeared suddenly, without warning. One minute you were in thick kiawe, the next you were climbing the shaking board steps of her house.

Inside it was very dark and airless. The dogs wiggled and wound about Lily's scratched shins. In a black corner, the mongoose lazily lifted its head from the straw basket where he was curled, stared without any emotion, then lowered his head back onto his paws. He was a nocturnal animal, but it was always dark inside. Fan lay on an old dining room table that was once Lily's mother's; on top of it were four or five mattresses. Like the princess and the pea, Lily thought. Under the dining table were cartons and burlap bags and cooking pots. Fan was smoking opium. A tiny brazier glowed under the table.

Tōsi squatted and waited. Fan motioned Lily to the side of the table. She slid nearer the edge to look into Lily's eyes, which were on the same level and only inches away.

"You sick, girl?" she asked.

"No."

She puffed her pipe.

"I'm thirsty," Lily said.

Behind her, Tōsi moved to get the gourd but a flicker of Fan's eyes stopped him.

"Why you so sad all the time," she said, not really asking but sighing. "When he brought her here, she was very unhappy. She is too much trouble. She should smoke like me." She gestured with the pipe and smiled. She had no teeth.

Lily did not know which woman Fan meant, Anna or Christmas, and she was afraid to ask. She was afraid that she might be telling a secret if she asked, "Christmas?"

A dog at Lily's feet yawned with that silly, high whine a dog makes. Fan was so close to her, Lily could smell her yellowness, that mysterious smell that white people do not have, and that yellow or brown people who live with whites lose. Lily thought it was like the smell of certain tree saps just as the nut began to rot. She loved the smell.

Lily coughed when she tried to speak and the words came out uneven and loud. "Where is my mother? Can you tell me?" She felt that awful ache in her jaw which was the strain and will not to weep.

Fan looked over Lily's shoulder and gestured nearly imperceptibly with her head and Tōsi moved behind Lily.

There was the sound of water being poured and he bumped into Lily in the dark and handed her a coconut shell of warm water. She drank it and began to cry, although she made no crying sound. Fan took the cup from her. She could barely keep her eyes open. She licked her purple lips.

"She is coming back," she said and she turned over and succumbed to her dreams.

It seemed like a long time before Lily felt Tōsi nudge her and then pull her gently to the curtained door. She stepped on a dog and then stumbled down the stairs. The sunlight was so bright that she covered her eyes with her hand. Tōsi led her back through the kiawe for a while, then she was able to make her own path, here and there, her nightgown snagging on branches, not bothering now to avoid the thorns, back through the dusty kiawe to the moist and lush garden edge, the garden and the forest like two different continents, two different planets. Then they crossed the croquet lawn and she didn't even bother to hold her gown above the dew.

Off the south verandah was the large room where Sheridan read and studied and gave Tōsi and Lily their lessons. It was filled with things he brought from the East when Lily was born. There were small and delicate bronze Buddhas with elongated ear lobes. Long stretches of antique silk and gold-threaded tapestry slid along black ebony tables, and an old bronze cooking cauldron with clawed feet sat in an open window. There were still chips of dried clay between the talons. There was a Buddha whose wooden crown twisted off. In the crown was an empty square hole where a jewel once fit, and in an opening in his back Lily once found pieces of red funeral paper, edges charred, smelling of ash and incense. The Buddha was freckled with traces of gold gilt. He was much more beautiful to Lily chipped and worn, red lacquer and gilt rubbed off, dry jewel hole empty, than he would have been when he was shining new gold and vermilion. Roman statues, blind and chalky and armless, seemed much more wonderful to her than they would have when they were painted bright colors and wore wigs and eyeglasses. She didn't think she would have liked the restored Angkor Wat as much as the creeper-tangled and decayed temple where her father said he had found the Buddha with the six arms.

As Lily passed along the verandah she saw Sheridan sitting in the room. He was not reading or working, just sitting there, so she went in. The hem of her nightgown was heavy and soaked with dew from the lawn. She held it up so that it would not drag on his floor. He looked at her but did not say anything. He was drinking green rice tea. He poured the clear, pale tea into a small, almost transparent, celadon cup and offered it to Lily with two hands. She took the cup and drank. There was almost no taste, only the vague odor of seaweed, a little salty and warm. "I thought you were sick," he said. "I was just coming to see you."

"I've been to see Fan. Tōsi took me to see her."

"And you're better now?" he asked. He was staring ahead, not looking at her, not thinking about her.

"I'm better."

"Good," he said suddenly, "because there's something I want to show you." He turned to her and smiled. She couldn't answer, she was thinking so hard about him, caught off guard by him, wishing now that she hadn't come into the room, but thinking that she loved him, Anna loved him. He had always been very good to her.

"They tell me you're ruining your eyes reading," he said.

"I don't think so."

"I suppose they think you should be outside."

"Why is everyone always talking about ruining my eyes?" she asked quietly. She felt a pain in her chest. It was difficult to exhale. She bent over a little to force out the air. He smiled at something, still preoccupied.

She wondered whether he was thinking about Christmas. It must be Christmas who wanted her outside, out of the house. She felt the teacup in her hands. She was afraid that she would crush it, eggshell-thin, in her two perspiring hands, but at the same time she couldn't put it down.

"It's just come. I've been waiting a long time for it. A missionary in Vientiane brought it out. Gave it to a Nationalist Chinese."

He pulled a mottled, gray and green bronze head of a god out of a small crate packed with torn newspaper. The newspaper was thin and bore character writing. He laid the head on the table. It could not stand on its own, torn as it must have been from some temple, dark and holy. He would have a new base for it made downtown.

"What do you think?" he asked after a long time.

"It's nice," she said timidly.

"It is. It's nice."

"And it's mysterious. It looks as though it should have a smell. I wonder how it got here."

"Through the jungle by pack? Rickshaw and sampan?"

"Pirates."

"I'm afraid it was a pilot for TWA."

She playfully put her hands over her ears.

"You prefer your version?"

"Sometimes."

"Well, you may." He picked up the head and held it fondly, examining it, squinting through his glasses, serious and far away.

"Fan has Mama's table," she said. Somehow the word slipped out. She had been trying not to say it: she said "Mama" and she started to shiver. She was afraid that her teeth would begin to chatter and make noise. She put the teacup down carefully, afraid that it too would make noise if she didn't get rid of it.

"Yes," he said and gently laid the head back in the crate. The print on the newspaper was smeared in places. Someone must have picked it up to read while the ink was still wet.

It probably left a stain on someone's fingers, she thought distractedly.

"Does she still have those animals?"

"Who?"

"Fan." He looked at her professionally over the top of his glasses. "Are you sure you're well?" He put his fingers on her wrist to take her pulse. "You could go into the hospital with me." He looked at his watch. "I have to see some patients at four, you could drive in with me."

"I feel fine," she said. "I am fine."

There were steps outside in the hall, flat, slap-sounding, barefoot. Whoever it was stopped at the door, waited, listened, then slapped away. He looked at his watch again. Lily knew it was Christmas who had stopped at the door.

"Your pulse is a little fast."

"What are you going to do?"

"I'll wait and see how you are this evening."

"No. When she comes back."

"Oh," he said. "I'll find her in the playroom. She likes the record player in the playroom." He stood up, brushing strips of paper from his lap. Lily wondered whether he was pretending not to understand that she was asking about Anna, not Christmas, or whether he didn't know himself what Fan had told her or whether Fan had told a lie: Anna wasn't coming back. He put his hands on her shoulders. She thought that he might hurt her, force her to take drugs, like Anna, from his black medical bag, or maybe he was going to hold her in his arms. Maybe this is what my mother feels, she thought; perhaps this is what it is like when you are crazy. Before she could find out, he turned away and went to find Christmas in the children's playroom.

Lily liked going to the hospital with her father. Sometimes Tōsi went too, and the nurses and orderlies would give them little things like wooden tongue depressors and rubber finger sheaths, and these presents became treasured, and splintered and stretched with play.

The wide corridors of Sheridan's wing had chairs down both sides, where the patients would wait. To walk down the hall with Sheridan was to be a courtier in the train of an emperor of some great exotic court. There were Chinese and Japanese and Samoans and Koreans and Hawaiians. Occasionally there would be a Caucasian, and Lily always noticed how red those faces were, slipped in between the cream and brown faces of the others. Many times patients would jump off their chairs when they recognized Sheridan and try to get his attention. They spoke in Pidgin English. They gave him gifts of fruit and preserved cracked-seed and salted plum. Lily and Tōsi were thrilled to be included in the adulation, but Sheridan did not like it. He had often asked the hospital to knock a door out of his office wall so that he could enter and leave unnoticed and the head engineer had promised to see to it, but the hospital privately liked the attention their doctor received.

Although it embarrassed Sheridan, he had grown used to it and no longer stopped to reassure the supplicants or graciously take the presents wrapped in newspaper and waxed paper that they held out to him. Lily and Tōsi were less modest, or less guilty-feeling perhaps, and were more than happy to keep the mangoes and leaf-wrapped sushi. Once they had been scolded by Sheridan for stuffing their pockets full of loot and he had not allowed them to accompany him to the hospital for a long time.

So Lily felt lucky to be asked, even though it was because he thought she might be sick. She asked whether Tōsi could come too and Sheridan, in a very good mood, thought it was a wonderful idea.

They waited for him in his office while he saw patients. They ate the almonds and lichees they had received when they made the royal procession through the hall.

Lily stared at the sharp black and white X-rays clipped to the lighted milk-glass panel behind her father's desk. One was of a head and there was an upper spine and perhaps an arm, or a leg. Her father could see through people, she thought.

The room was extremely spare and clean. Unlike his rooms at home, it held no extraordinary Buddha heads or long scrolls of calligraphy. There were only medical books and chairs with a strong smell of leather. There was also a table with instruments and there was a sink. Lily marveled at the difference between the way her father lived here and the way he lived at home. His room at the hospital was like a priest's cell. It was so superficially devoid of what would have been called personality that the sense of its occupant was far stronger than if it had been crowded with personal mementos. Sheridan did not even have the customary framed degrees and awards on the walls.

Lily felt comfortable sitting at her father's desk. She thought the room was serene, an oasis, the opposite of his lush cloth-of-gold kimonos and the opposite, even, of her mother. She understood why he used it as a refuge. Everything was in order. There would be no sudden surprises. No matter what happened he would know what to do. It was not like that at the Big House.

"Fan does the I Ching," Tōsi said, watching Lily carefully. "Maybe she does know."

Lily shrugged listlessly. "What if she's dead? I think about that all the time. That she is dead and buried." She stared again at the X-rays. "She would look like that by now, just bones inside a pair of shoes. It's been twenty-nine days."

Tōsi went behind the desk to switch off the light panel.

"You'd better not," she said wearily. "He doesn't like us to touch anything."

He nodded solemnly. He sat down again, wiping the almond sugar from his hands onto the back of his shorts. Sometimes, when they were less worried, they would lean across Sheridan's big, bare desk and leaf slowly through the books with the florid color photographs of tumors and hydrocephalic infants and amputations, but they were too preoccupied now. When Anna first disappeared, the children thought she might be in Sheridan's hospital and they telephoned perhaps twenty times, badly disguising their voices. They asked for Anna in every possible variation of her name. They said that it was urgent, they were calling long distance (nostrils held tightly closed with fingers), but the operator always said no, she had not been admitted.

The door opened and Sheridan came in, calm and relaxed. He was not worried or preoccupied, but his best self, his healer self. He flicked off the light illuminating the X-rays. "Bad humerus fracture," he said to himself. So it was an arm, Lily thought. Sheridan had taught them the names of every bone and muscle in the body the way some children are taught state capitals.

Tōsi sat up attentively in his chair. He loved Sheridan. He never missed a word he said, or a gesture or an expression. He, like Lily, recognized that Sheridan was not without fault, but this awareness did not trouble him as it troubled Lily. He was not ill at ease with ambiguity. Perhaps it was the result of not being raised a Catholic. He did not divide the world and everything in it into good and bad. To do so, as Lily was compelled to do, led to confusion and suffering. What was she to think when she discovered that almost everything, including and most important, her mother and her father, consisted of both? She had not been taught otherwise, or been benignly neglected in her religious instruction like Tōsi, and she was too young to have reasoned and understood for herself. That would take years. Tōsi did not make distinctions between good and bad and he had no need for explanations and reasons when he found them lodged happily together. It gave him an advantage over Lily.

"I have one short lecture," Sheridan said, "and then we can go. You look fine to me, Lily." He handed a medical journal across the desk to them. "No bloody pictures today?" He smiled. Lily and Tōsi looked at each other. Their medical reading had been a secret. Behind her father, the X-rays were just cold, gray squares. He can see through people, she thought again.

EIGHT

ᗩ ESTERDAY I wrote to the San Francisco lawyers. I was
curious as to what business my father had had with
them before he disappeared. I hope it will give us a clue. I
also wrote to Jack, although I'm not sure he'll get the letter —
I have only a six-month-old address for him on a lake in
Kashmir. I want him to know about Tōsi. He too must have
wondered over the years. It was Jack who found the picture
of Father on the bridge in Hiroshima when his hair went
white overnight.

When I returned from my walk to the mailbox in the
village, I could see Anna waiting for me in the tall mustard
grass, absent-mindedly scratching the mosquito bites on her
ankles and wrists. She scratched them all at once, so it looked
as if she were dancing.

She ran jerkily to meet me and as we walked back across
the lawn, she began her customary litany of questions: Am I
going to die? Will Jessie come back? Where is Papa?

When I said that Papa was in California, she nodded and

passed on to the next question (was Tōsi old?) and I watched carefully to see whether her nonchalance was real. She does not like it when I am too serious. It worries her.

It occurred to me that the answers to her questions do not matter, as the questions do not even matter, so much as the ritual of drawing me out of myself and back into the world. But ever since her father sent her a wooden doll from Russia that twists open to reveal ten more wooden dolls, smaller and smaller, each hidden inside another, she has asked many, many times whether we can talk about how cold it is in Russia. I wonder about this question. Is it like a dream pun? Does she think the world is chilling?

I have long since run out of serious and thoughtful answers about the Russian winter, once even resorting to an encyclopedia I gratefully discovered in a hotel reading room, so I have now turned it into a game. When I tell her that it is so cold that the children have to wear Wellingtons on their noses, she shakes with thick, drunken laughter.

"How cold is it in Russia, Mother?"

"Well," I said, thinking. She ran ahead so that she could turn to face me, beginning to laugh already, happy and twitching.

"It's sooooo cold in Russia, the polar bears sleep with electric blankets." She rocked heavily with her deep, sailor laugh.

Tōsi came out of the house. He was smiling as though he too were imagining polar bears and blankets and miles and miles of extension cord. He said "Anna-san" fiercely and clapped once, crossing his hands at the wrist. With two quick elegant leaps, Anna was sitting on his shoulders, grinning. I was quite startled. He was always teaching her little things. He is rather like Sheridan, I thought. Anna and he were thrilled with themselves. Perhaps they had been practicing extra hard for this trick.

"Anna!" I said. We went inside. "How did you do that?" She was very proud, and pretending not to be, looking at her accomplice and winking broadly once or twice.

"I want to talk to both of you," I said.

There was no reason that Anna should fear my having to talk to them, but perhaps I looked worried, because she immediately slid lumpily down Tōsi's back, forgetting the graceful moves he had taught her. Tōsi too looked full of anxiety. They made me nervous.

"I'm going to my grandmother's," I said quickly. "Anna, you and Tōsi will visit your father in California. I'll meet you there." They just looked at me, dumbfounded.

"I'm coming back. I promise." I sounded harsh even to myself. Then I remembered the night in my room with Jack and Jessie and Tōsi when our mother went away.

I sat down and took Anna on my lap. She already had her thumb in her mouth. "You know I'll come back," I said. She didn't answer. Tōsi excused himself to make tea, his own form of withdrawal, away from friendship and back into servitude.

Anna snuggled into my chest. Tōsi came back with the tea tray, solemn and precise. I leaned around Anna for my tea and drank with an artificial smacking of my lips and a feigned pleasure. I felt very self-conscious. I was not as comfortable with my decision to visit my grandmother as I pretended to be. Once, they could have easily bullied me until I took them along, but for some reason I had the unfamiliar feeling that I was doing the right thing. Not since I was a child, twelve years old to be exact, the night my mother asked me to do something for her, have I ever felt that what I was doing was right. I haven't thought it was wrong, either. I just happened to lose, that evening when my mother came into my room, the ability to judge my own actions.

❧

I had written to the San Francisco lawyers another time, eight years ago. It was when I first went to my grandmother's in Philadelphia and decided that my father did not care about me, because if he did he would not have let me go, and decided further that he was a man who could not care about anyone. I wrote to ask that they not send me any more money.

I had only the cash from the refunded airline ticket and, from Tigger, the name of a man who owned a newspaper. In the hurried half-hour I had spent with Tigger at the Big House while I packed (taking mostly my mother's hand-me-downs for my new city life), she had given me the name of the only person she knew in Philadelphia, someone whom I was to call. It would be suitable to lunch with him if he asked me. He was an older gentleman, she had said, flicking a piece of tobacco off the tip of her finger with a long, red nail. "Be sure to give him my love," she said twice. "He owns newspapers and things."

So I called Tigger's friend, Mr. Wallenberg. He invited me to lunch and I went, a long-limbed teen-ager in a Chanel suit. He was surprised that I was so young. Disappointed was the word he used. He asked after Tigger and chuckled fondly. He had spent time with Tigger in Nevada, he said, while he was doing some legal work. I was too dumb to realize he meant divorce. Tigger walked her little dog across the Hoover Dam every day for six weeks, he said. He was very nice. He held my hand in both of his and asked what would make me happy. I was embarrassed, but I admitted that I wanted to be a reporter. He squeezed my hand and told me to go to the personnel office at his newspaper the next day.

The personnel office, obviously having been sent many lunch friends of Mr. Wallenberg's, simply directed me downstairs. Before I knew it, I was sitting, not at the city desk as I had imagined, but in a chair on wheels in a tiny, stifling hot cubicle. There was an electric typewriter and a headset. Behind the typewriter was an open trough. To my bewilderment, I had somehow become a classified-ad taker.

I sat on my rolling chair in my tiny stall and took advertisements over the telephone. When I had typed one, I ripped it from the typewriter and threw it into the moving trough already bobbing with the ripped-off sheets of the sixty other ad takers. It was summer and it was very hot. Once, I fainted and was allowed to lie down in my mother's Balenciaga voile dress on the dusty cot in the woman employees' lounge.

The one thing that made me happy was that it was not dark when I came out of the big newspaper building every evening. I took the subway home to my grandmother. I slept on my day off. I made a few friends. They thought I was different, hard to peg, they said, and asked me things like "Did you live in a grass shack?" and "Do they speak English in Hawaii?" I had boy friends. I wrote to Tōsi. I was in a daze.

I also got into trouble. I was supposed to be making money for the newspaper. If some old man called in, wanting to sell his last chair for twenty dollars, I had been instructed to say: "Wonderful, soft, comfortable chair for immediate sale, good for your tired back. Please call Mr. Grover Jefferson at 650-2222 night or day and work out a price that suits us both." But I would feel sorry for Mr. Jefferson and advise him to buy an ad that read "Chair. $20. 650-2222." The supervisor listened in on the calls and I was caught. The third time it happened, I was fired. Perhaps it was rude, but I didn't bother to say good-bye to Mr. Wallenberg.

My next job was with an advertising agency. The agency represented a big metals company. The director of the company was in the office one day while I was bringing mugs of coffee to the ad executives and he looked at me and said, "What about her?" That is how I became Miss Aluminum.

I wore a dress with a mermaid tail in the back, all made of aluminum, and I carried an aluminum trident. I wore an aluminum-foil tiara. They took me to New York to appear at a lunch for the owners of big yachts who might be interested in constructing the hulls of their next boats out of aluminum. The lunch was at "21." I had to walk through the crowded restaurant wearing my metal dress and carrying my trident. Naturally, people stared. They even giggled. I did not make it through the lunch, but left my special aluminum throne at the head of the table and ran crying to the back of the restaurant. A man who had been at a nearby table, and who had been staring at me with what I thought was amusement, came after me and comforted me. He wiped my face and took off the tiara and laid it on a plate. He was an Italian named Ludovico Anchinelli. He had not been staring at me with mockery, he said, but with sympathy. He gently walked me through the restaurant, past the open-mouthed yachtsmen, and out into the street. I saw that he was not embarrassed to be with me.

It was my first serious romance. I went to Italy. I moved to New York. I had other boy friends. Ludovico stayed with me when he was there. He was sophisticated and indulgent. I was not unhappy, although if I heard island music in the night or smelled island flowers through the walls, I would begin to cry. I could not go to Trader Vic's.

It was like that for a long time. I missed my mother. I was vacant and vague. I was unpredictable. Ludovico gave up. Others gave up. Then when I became pregnant and would not get married, I wrote once more to the San Francisco lawyers. The money that I had refused for five years was untouched. Because of Sheridan's customary scrupulosity, it had accumulated. I asked for the money. I sent a ticket to Tōsi in Japan. He arrived one month before little Anna was born. I did not know then that he had been given to Anna, my mother, one month before I was born.

And we have been together, the three of us, ever since. I have not had any boy friends. I know this is not as it should be, but I don't know how to begin again. I have become too comfortable in my solitude. I don't know whether I would like anyone else in my bed in the morning. My nun's pallet, I call it. I don't know how to fix things, how to go back, or rather, how to go forward. When Anna was born I seemed to become the child she was, reunited with Tōsi, dreaming on islands, in the ocean every day, without a sense of time passing, and with no concerns other than getting to the top of the bluff in time to see the summer sunset. Anna's father says it is an attempt to re-create an idealized childhood. He, too, has given up. I would like to change. I do not want to harm my Anna but I wonder whether it is possible to make it right. I used to want to make it all right for my mother, but I did not know how then either.

☙

My grandmother and my Aunt Helen live in the same North Philadelphia row house where my mother was born. It was once a lively, noisy neighborhood of Irish and Polish immigrants, with a drugstore on one corner and a two-chair barber shop on the other. Now my grandmother and Aunt Helen are one of the last two white families on the street. The tiny houses, already run-down and dirty, are being bought by blacks, and the street is eerily quiet, eerie because my relatives have always said that Negroes were loud. Only one car at a time can go down the long one-way street, so people park their cars on the pavement with two wheels in the street.

When we were very young, my mother told us lovely stories about her childhood: how they lived in a huge mansion named Old Oaks, with white pillars on the top of a green hill and how they had the first refrigerator in the state of Pennsylvania. I knew soon enough that she was lying, but it wasn't until I was there in the little row house that I realized she had taken the stories from her own mother, who must have told her children, huddled around a low coal fire, about the rich people for whom she worked. It shamed my mother that they were poor. It did not shame me, but then I had not had to wear newspapers under my skirts in winter.

So back in that little house, overheated now and safe from the autumn chill, I, in turn, sat at my grandmother's feet and asked for stories, real stories. I wanted to know about Anna and Sheridan. I wanted to know everything there was to know. Sometimes I even interrupted her to find a piece of brown grocery bag and a broken-off pencil to write something down.

It was exhausting for Gagi, and once she cried, wiping her old eyes, so old that it made my eyes water to look into them. She wiped her pink face with the handkerchief embroidered with the shamrocks, with the rosary beads inside, so that the handkerchief made noise when she used it. Helen, sitting across the tiny room reading the evening newspaper, peered around the side of the paper and made a face at me to stop asking so many questions, it was too upsetting. Aunt Helen herself would not answer my questions. "I don't want to talk about it," she said.

"But what do you think was wrong with my mother?" I asked my grandmother.

She waved her swollen, veined hand. I realized that she was already old when I was a child.

"She was always an odd little thing," she said. She stopped and took the television schedule from her knitting basket.

"That's right," my aunt said. " 'The Brady Bunch.' " I didn't know how she could see so much from behind her paper. Now I would have to wait until the next day.

At our five-thirty dinners, Aunt Helen acted as though I were hastening her mother's death. I realized that I did feel as if I were losing time. I was in a hurry.

"You know that Father has disappeared," I said, as if in explanation. Helen just shrugged and kept on chewing. Gagi moved her lips as though she were praying, not eating. I realized later that her false teeth made her do it.

We went to bed early, too. The sky was still pale. The stars did not come out until we had been in bed for hours. I lay sleepless in the old tin bed where my mother was born. I watched the small moon rise through the dusty Venetian blinds. The bed was wide and short. I could stretch out my arms, but my feet hung over the end. The springs were broken and made a loud noise if I even turned my head on the pillow. I knew the sound woke Helen, lying in the next room, long, freckled arms folded across her dry chest. She would cough and have trouble getting back to sleep. I had upset their little household by coming. But as with Tōsi and Anna when they wanted to come with me, I would not be dissuaded. I did not mean to be selfish. I resented their moral squeamishness, their refusal to think about Anna. I was not trying to finish my grandmother off, as Helen had accused me the first night. I was, to use one of her own expressions, getting it out of my system.

In the morning, when my aunt was at work and Gagi was newly rested, I brought her weak tea and cinnamon toast and sat on the floor near her rocker. I liked waiting on her. She had had a very hard life taking care of other people. I forced myself to be patient while she noisily ate her breakfast. She understood why I was there. She did not torture me unnecessarily. She had taken years to put these things out of her mind, by determination and prayer, and now I was asking her to recall them in detail.

"I always felt sorry for him," she said suddenly. "He didn't have a chance."

"With her, you mean?"

She shrugged with a vague contempt. "The War finished him off. He used to say that the world ended in 1945."

"The year I was born." She didn't hear me.

"For a long time, maybe a year, maybe longer, she refused to bring him home. She was ashamed. I understood, I could see why. My lady used to say to me 'Rose, you were never meant to wait on me.' Millicent Wagner wouldn't put on a stitch of clothing that I hadn't laid out for her." She shook her finger at me.

There was a clang as the mail slot in the front door was flipped open and a few envelopes were poked through. They slowly dropped one by one to the worn rug. I brought them over for her. They were nothing but solicitations from religious orders for more money. She didn't look at them.

"I sat at this very window and watched him wander up and down this street, with the address on a piece of paper in his hand, looking for the house, and she, who had been dressed and waiting since seven o'clock that morning, wouldn't let me call out to him. She sat beside me here and watched him for over half an hour." She smiled. She had worshiped Anna. As mothers sometimes do, she had groomed and schooled and clipped Anna to be her vindication. In some ways, she had succeeded very well. When she was finished with her, her "lady" could have laid out Anna's clothes. Even I could readily remember that Anna had been magnificent.

"She loved me, but she would not bring him home to meet me. I never insisted. She finally did but she told him" — she shook her head fondly — "she told him it would be easy to find. It was the one with the white pillars."

I looked out the window at the endless row of peeled and stripped pillars on both sides of the street.

"Like the mansion on the hill?" I asked. "Sheridan was looking for a rich man's house?" It seemed very cruel. She was smiling, even though it had been cruel to her as well. To my surprise, I took my father's side. "And what did he do?" I was indignant for him. It had been foolish of Anna as well as cruel.

"Nothing."

He must not have cared, I thought. She had misled him for a year. He never minded, but he never understood why she had needed to lie, or he would never have taken her away to an island where her position, her wealth, her glory, meant nothing because she was a stranger. In the end, my grandmother's efforts were meaningless. How could it matter if the sisters from the convent school were not there to see it? Worst of all, if Gagi was not there to share in it herself?

It is also possible that Father was more clever than they realized. Perhaps that was one of the reasons he chose the islands. Perhaps he, in turn, had misled them. He had no intention of having the kind of life Anna had been schooled for by her eager mother.

"He liked me, you know," she said dreamily. I saw that she was drifting away. I stood up to carry her breakfast dishes into the kitchen.

"You're so like her," she said, gazing at me from under her lids, her head back against the chair, her old neck stretched nearly smooth.

The dishes rattled in my hands. "I am?"

"The spitting image."

"I hope this doesn't offend you, but I don't think that I am like her. I don't *want* to be like her. That's why I'm here and bothering you with all these questions. I don't want to be like her."

She lifted her head off the chair and looked at me for a long time, then she turned to stare out into the ugly street.

"I know what you mean."

"You do?"

"I never liked her legs much." She looked back at me. "Too shapely," she said.

I took the dishes to the kitchen and began to laugh. I decided that it was time for me to leave.

"Do you want to come with me?" I called from the kitchen. "I can take care of you."

"No," I heard her say.

The afternoon that I was leaving, struggling with my bag on the steep, narrow staircase, I suddenly felt happy. I gave my bag a good push at the top and it bounced to the bottom without much harm. My grandmother was in the rocker by the window.

"You told her about the girl friend," she said placidly. I was not sure I had heard her correctly. If I had, it sounded surprisingly malicious. Perhaps she is angry that I came, I thought, or angry that I am leaving.

"I told her?" I said, shocked. "*I* told her?"

"That's what she said. Years ago."

"What's the matter with this family? Didn't you ever teach her to take responsibility for her own actions? You only taught her how to dress? Did you ever think about consequences?" I was very angry. "How could *I* have told her?"

"You were there. You saw everything." She did not attach any moral significance to what she had just said and I realized that she had not, the whole week long, attached moral significance to anything. For her, it was simply information. I felt myself become a little hysterical, wanting to force her to have a point of view, an opinion, to say that I was not to blame. But she was incapable of that because she had never seen it as a matter of blame. How could she absolve me from some imagined mortal sin, committed ten years earlier, on an island thousands of miles away in the middle of an ocean? She had not even been there. No one but me ever thought that I was responsible for my mother.

"Why didn't she leave then?" I shouted at my grandmother. She looked at me, surprised and a little impatient. "Why did she stay?" I asked, forcing my voice down, but still shrill and whining.

"Because," she said coldly, "he told her he would take you children away from her." She stared out the window. The taxicab had pulled up in front and the driver honked loudly. I was confused. She sighed and impatiently turned back to me. "Because of her history, the institution and the drugs, he could have taken you from her."

"That's horrible!" I felt like screaming. I held my jaws together tightly.

"That's just what she said," and she smiled, sweetly satisfied that I had finally proved her right. "Your mother's words *exactly!*"

NINE

LATE ONE MORNING, without any fuss or warning, their mother came home. They all gathered around her on the front steps, nuzzling and whooping under her arms and in her hair. She had gained a little weight, and there was a long, open sore down the side of her face, close to the hairline, angling at her jaw and running under what she would have called her big mick chin. With Jessie and Jack butting and nudging her like tug boats, Lily and Tōsi took Anna by her hands and drew her up the steps into the house.

After the first thrill of seeing her, Lily suddenly felt a shock as sharp and strong as a toothache: perhaps Christmas was in the house. She waited until Anna was distracted before she backed nonchalantly out of the room. Out of sight, she raced to the back of the house where Christmas lived. Lily had never been in her room before. For the past few weeks, she had not even wanted to be near that part of the house. She didn't stop to knock, but flung open the door noisily and stopped short inside, panting and angry. The room was empty.

Christmas was gone. The room was bare except for an empty greeting-card box on the floor. Lily sat down on the clean, stripped mattress to get her breath. She felt that Christmas was lucky. She had felt, running through the house, that she would kill Christmas.

She ran back to her mother. She knew Anna would miss her. They were all in her small sitting room, Jessie and Jack crowded on either side of her on the rose-colored sofa while Tōsi ran in and out of the bedroom, overseeing the preparation of the bed, as she must rest and not get too excited.

"Where is Father?" Lily asked loudly.

"At the hospital," Anna said and smiled at her, motioning for her to come and squeeze onto the sofa with them. Lily blushed.

She sat on the sofa arm, above Jessie, who nestled in Anna's side. Anna shyly stroked Lily's face. Lily sensed how nervous and embarrassed Anna felt. Lily could hear Tōsi in the next room, rearranging the bedside table once again. Anna's room was filled with the fresh flowers Tōsi had gathered and put there every morning since she went away. The fragrance of tuberose and pakalana had filled the house for weeks. Her room had been kept ready by Tōsi, but he was too excited to relinquish it now that she had returned.

"Tōsi knew you would come back," Jack said quietly.

"I hope so," she said. She suddenly looked very sad.

"I didn't," Jessie said. "I didn't know."

"My poor baby. My sweet, sweet children," she said passionately and took Jessie in her arms. Lily slid off the arm onto the sofa, and Anna held her tightly too, Lily's head in Jessie's hair. Anna rocked back and forth gently.

"My old sweethearts," she said.

Lily could feel the weeping-ache begin in her jaw. "There's been a *lot* of crying around here," she said.

"Oh, my old sweethearts," Anna said again, still rocking.

"I love you, Mama," Lily said, trying not to cry, squeezed between her and Jessie, almost in Anna's lap, which is where they all wanted to be. "How did you get that sore?" Lily whispered. It was red and scabious down her soft pale face. Flecks of dried skin and blood stuck in the light down on her cheek. She put her shaking hand up to hide it.

"Oh, I'm ashamed to say."

"It's not so bad."

"I am ashamed to say it's from rubbing."

Lily felt sick and ashamed, too. Anna had rubbed the skin off one side of her face. "Don't touch it, Mama." Lily pulled her hand down.

Tōsi began unpacking her bag in the other room. Lily heard the heavy snap-sound as he released the spring catches. She always liked that sound, journeys begun and journeys ended.

"I told you, didn't I?" Anna said suddenly and quietly to Lily. She had tears in her eyes and she looked at Lily closely, trying to read her mind. She was sitting up stiff, her whole self taut and anxious.

"Told me? Told me what?"

"I know I did," she said. She relaxed her body and shuddered back against the sofa, her head against the mirror on the wall behind the sofa. She shook her head slowly from side to side and the tears came down her face. "Oh, Mama," Jessie and Jack said, almost in unison, and they too began to cry, although they would not have known whether it was for happiness or sorrow. She wiped her face with a great effort to control herself and she pulled the two younger children off her breast and said, "You know what would make me very, very happy? Your father told me there were some new pigeon eggs. Would you bring them to me?" Jessie and Jack got up, faces wet and dazed, and moved off slowly, as if in a dream, sniffling and nodding.

Anna watched them until they were out of sight, then she sighed and shivered and held Lily's hand. Lily noticed two small marks on either side of her mother's temples. It reminded her of the forceps indentations she had once seen on the head of a newborn baby.

"Oh, Lily, can you forgive me? I told you. I told you everything. I told you and I shall never be able to undo it, the stupid messiness of it."

"Mama," Lily said, starting to cry. "Please stop it. From my heart of hearts, I beg you." It was terrifying to cry: Lily could feel the hysteria sidling up on her, sly and steady. If she ever really started, she thought, she would never be able to stop, not her whole life long. Anna lifted Lily's head and looked at her and wiped the tears from her face with the hem of her dress. Anna was trembling.

"It didn't work, you see. What they did to me didn't work. I was supposed to forget everything, it would be like starting fresh, a state of grace again, like you, you are in a state of grace, Lily. It is what I longed for, why I went. Only I didn't forget. I remembered. And I remember so clearly: I got you out of your bed night after night. I let you see too much."

"Oh, Mama." Lily sobbed. "You didn't."

She just shook her head and laid it back again on the mirror, not letting go of Lily's hand, not looking at her, knowing Lily was lying. Anna withdrew, detached herself from the girl, from the house, from the smell of jasmine and tuberose. She couldn't help it.

Lily got up, stiff and cold, and went into the bedroom for a handkerchief. Tōsi was almost finished. He laid Anna's black Chinese pajamas on the bed. He looked up automatically, not out of interest, when Lily came in. He didn't see

Lily when Anna was around. They were all like that about her. "Ready now," he said happily.

"Mama," Lily called, and they both went to get her to bring her in to bed.

❧

Now that Anna was back, Jack ended his retreat and returned to school. She spent one morning alone with him on the boat and when they came in, he neatly rearranged his schedule: the gardener was to resume cleaning the pigeon coops, and his orchid seedlings were returned to the greenhouse.

Anna, however, had to go to school with him. She spent her mornings in the sandbox outside his classroom, smoking and reading, occasionally looking up to let him know that she was alert and paying attention. She had trouble with her cigarette butts, no ashtrays having been provided; and not wanting to leave them in the sandbox for the teachers to see, she filled her pockets with butts, often forgetting to empty them. She smelled, during this period, like damp sand and ash.

For the first two days, Jack stood at the window and watched her. Every so often she smiled exaggeratedly, so that he could see, and gave a big wave, but he remained at the window, unconvinced and expressionless. Eventually, when she realized that she wasn't going to leave, he began to join the other children in learning numbers and spelling but he still returned to the window every fifteen minutes to see whether she was still there. She was reading a new book, *Bonjour Tristesse*, the perfect book for a sandbox, she said.

As time went by, she was able to get up and walk around, to stretch her legs and throw her butts in the bushes, always careful to remain in view of the window, where he would appear only every hour now. Then, after discussing it with him, she was able to leave for short periods, walking up to the lily pond, or across the road to the Korean store for a paper cup of shaved ice and syrup. She could not be gone long. She allowed herself only a few minutes, then hurried back to her post.

Tigger picked them up one Friday afternoon after school. Jack held Anna's hand. She was gay and happy to see Tigger.

"Gosh!" she said happily as she put Jack into the back of the car with Lily and climbed into the front.

"Let's stop at the hotel," Tigger said. "Celebrate. It's the end of the school week for you, sugar."

Anna held her shoes out the window and shook out the sand.

The hotel was not far. It was a lacy, white Victorian mansion on the beach and had once been a king's palace. During the War, American officers lived there and it had been a lovely place to go to dance. Tigger remembered it as the best time of her life.

There was a terrace with an old Indian banyan in the center with small tables under its branches. Sometimes the banyan roots dangled over the tables. In the afternoons, an orchestra played old songs on the verandah. Anna often took the children there to have cocktails and to watch the sun slide into the ocean.

"You missed some swell parties, sugar. It was a lovely cruise."

"I'm sure I did," Anna said.

They walked through the hotel to the beach. Tigger kept her narrowed eyes on Anna, afraid Anna was mocking her, but Anna just smiled amiably and Tigger nearly bumped into a waiter. "Careful, sugar," Anna said and smiled.

"Well, let me tell you, Mary Kinney had her annual barbecue, you know, the one she has every year where the ladies go in chiffon and diamonds and I went the first year in blue

138

jeans and boots because, after all, the engraved invitation said 'barbecue' clear as day! Well! This year it was placéed! Can you imagine! They'd be turning over in Brownsville. Everyone asked for you. I said you were in California."

"I thought you came from 'just outside Dallas.' "

Tigger stopped, but Anna just looked ahead and kept walking.

"Well," Tigger said, "it certainly beats the booby hatch!"

Anna smiled and said, "It probably does."

They saw some women they knew and stopped to talk, and Jack and Lily waited on the side, shuffling and patient. Lily felt awkward in front of people. She had felt this way for a while, since the night of Sheridan's party when she had fainted. She thought that her hands and feet were too big for her body. Anna said good-bye to the women, and the captain ushered Anna ahead and pulled out her chair, then Tigger's, and they sat down.

"This *is* a special treat," Anna said. She squeezed Jack's hand. He had not taken his eyes away from her.

"Could I interrupt you two lovebirds to ask what you want to drink?" Tigger asked.

"Oh, rum collins, fruit punch for the children. Pack of cigarettes, no filter."

"Is that all?"

"Should be," Anna said calmly. There was always a mild struggle between them. Tigger seemed unusually frustrated. It made Lily nervous. Anna's hand went to the pale pink scar line on her face. She struggled not to touch it.

"Why don't you kids go and play on the beach," Tigger said.

They looked at Anna. "They're all right," she said. Tigger shrugged. She was annoyed.

"If you don't mind, I don't mind," she said.

The drinks came. The band returned from its break and played "Marie." Anna hummed along.

"That girl lives right around the corner. A few blocks from here, near Kuhio Beach," Tigger said. She sipped her drink through a straw, not looking up. "That's where he put her." She let the straw drop out of her mouth and a thin strand of saliva made a bridge from the straw to her lip.

"I don't think it matters," Anna said quietly, humming louder.

"All right, sugar," said Tigger, shrugging. "Only I thought that's what friends were for." She was elaborately nonchalant.

Anna lifted Jack up by one hand and Lily by the other, and pushed back their chairs with a loud, scraping noise. They left the terrace and went quickly through the cool lobby and out under the porte-cochère and stumbled into a taxi that still smelled of the leis the last passengers had worn in from the airport. She held their hands all the way home.

When they arrived she sent Lily in to get some money for the taxi. She never had money. Lily had once seen her write a check for ice cream. Lily got the money from Tōsi, and Anna paid the Portuguese taximan. Jack went off to see his pigeons. She put her arm around Lily and they went inside.

"Would you stay with me a little while?" she asked. Lily was pleased and embarrassed, that a mother would have to ask. "Of course," she said, and in her awkwardness she snorted air out of her nose. Anna squeezed her arm and they walked through the house, across the cool, shiny floors to the room off the gallery where Lily used to sit at Anna's desk and watch Christmas dance.

The gallery was empty. Anna lay on her side against a huge pile of pillows on the big sofa covered with old Indonesian ikats. She lit a cigarette and held her arm stretched straight to the ceiling. She seemed to forget that she had the cigarette. It burned slowly, giving off white smoke, in the air above her. She looked up at the smoke finally and brought her arm down.

"She was here, wasn't she?"

"Who?" Lily knew who.

"Christmas. Your father brought her here when I was in the hospital. She was here in this house, perhaps in this room." She looked around the room curiously, as if she hoped to find proof, or a clue, or something altered and out of place.

"She was never in this room," Lily said. Now Anna looked at Lily.

"Did you like her?"

"Oh, Mother." Lily moaned.

Anna sat up quickly. "I'm sorry, child. You need not speak. I cannot help it. I want to know everything and it is killing me. No one will tell me. Not even Tōsi. They have some strange idea that it is better not to know, but it is the not knowing that makes me crazy." She spoke in a whisper. "I am sorry I asked, brought it up even, but it is all I think about. Please forgive me."

"Tigger would tell you."

She nodded and fell back on the pillows. "This is not how I imagined it would be."

"I'll tell you," Lily said. "I'll tell you and I'll do anything you want." She slid down next to her mother. She felt worn out and sad. Anna ran her fingers idly up and down the pale inside of Lily's arm.

"I know. I know." Anna shuddered.

They stayed that way for a long time, Anna tickling Lily's arm and smoking and still looking all around the room, Lily staring at her, her fingers twitching now and then, while the

house around them creaked and hummed with children and
servants and tame animals.

⌒⅔

Ishi, the gardener, had left a message for Lily that the new
phalaenopsis had budded. She went through the orchard to the
greenhouse. She was happy. The cattleyas would be blooming,
and although Lily knew Anna thought them the more vulgar
orchid, she would pick her a big, scentless, purple one. Lily
loved the dirt smell of the greenhouse. She walked down the
long aisle, blooming phalaenopsis arching above her on both
sides, white like brides, with a fleck of purple-red in their cen-
ters. Moisture dripped and slid down the glass walls. It was
very quiet. There was only the smell of humus. Lily thought
it must smell like that in a grave. She hoped it smelled like
that.

She was at the far end examining the tiny hybrid seedlings
in their beds, so she did not hear them come in. Not until one
of them knocked over or threw down a clay pot that thudded in the hard dirt did she know that they were there, and for
some reason she did not call out or show herself but crouched
down behind a tub of weeping birch Sheridan was trying to
grow in the tropics.

Lily could see Anna through the leaves. Her mouth looked
large and red in all the milk and green. She could not see her
father. He must have bent down to pick up the pot.

"I am trying my hardest," Anna said. "It is not my fault
that the treatments did not work."

He stood up. Lily could see the back of his head. She could
not hear what he said. He always spoke so quietly.

"But I could not go through it again." Anna pulled the hair
back tightly from her forehead with both hands and he took

142

her hands and pulled them down. "I miss my mother," Anna whispered. He turned away, toward Lily.

"You won't have to go back," he said. He went a few steps from her and she came up quickly behind him.

"You must never see her again."

He stepped away again. "We've already spoken about that."

"But I must believe you, if I don't believe you, if I don't know it, I can't go on —"

"I've told you. I've told you again and again."

"I'm sorry," she said pitifully. He turned back to her, smiling, and put his arm around her shoulder like a friend and squeezed her a little.

"Don't be so pathetic."

"It is so difficult for me to understand why. I know you say that it has nothing to do with me, but I don't see how it *can* have nothing to do with me, it *must* have something to do with me, it *should* have something to do with me." She was becoming frantic. She knocked over another clay pot with her elbow and spun around as it fell and broke, trying to catch it. "I'm sorry!" she said. He grabbed her fluttering hands.

It was very hot. Lily was moist and weak, hiding behind the trembling birch tree. She could not come out now. She had pins and needles in one leg. With no warning, a camellia broke soundlessly from a branch nearby and landed next to her in the dirt and frightened her. They walked toward her. If they found her, she thought quickly, she would pretend that she was dead.

He held her mother's wrists in one hand, at his side. She looked like a prisoner, only she stared at him so strangely, like an ecstatic prisoner. She did not pull her hands away, but when they reached the narrow aisle and could not continue abreast, she turned so that he was caught between her and the trembling sprays of flowers. Still holding her wrists, he encircled her quivering throat with his other hand and tightened it around her throat and kissed her. She moaned.

Lily felt very strange. She closed her eyes tight. Now she had pins and needles all over her body and she was afraid that she, too, would make a noise. She wanted to moan like Anna. When she could not help herself and raised her head to look, she could not see them. She heard a low cry but she could not tell whether it was her mother or her father. Perhaps she could crawl on her stomach down the other aisle. They might not notice, being so busy, and she could escape and leave them alone in the wet heat. But she could not move. She closed her eyes again. She was afraid now that she would see them. There was the sound of her mother's breathing, and he said something, and then she moaned again and it was quiet.

A long time passed. When Lily lifted her head from the dirt and opened her eyes, dizzy and green and sudsy, they were done and gone.

Anna celebrated all holidays with great fervor. Five or six times a year, when she was there, all of her energy and imagination were concentrated on fireworks and bunnies and Christmas angels and pumpkin pies, holidays grown from old rites of summer solstice and human sacrifice and the rising of the dead, all celebrated on a hot, wet, overgrown island where no one had ever dreamed of snow or leaves changing color, let alone seen them, especially not the children, whose early fantasies were originated and kept alive by her alone. So it seemed perfectly natural to them, although it must have seemed odd to some of their country neighbors and certainly to the native islanders, to see each hot December a man dressed in a heavy red wool suit with a thick white beard and high black boots climbing over the roof of the Big House with a big sack, drop-ping soap flakes over the side so that from the dining room, Christmas Eve, it looked to those happily gathered there as if it were snowing.

That Hallowe'en she decided to go out with the children. Weeks were spent planning their costumes. Jessie dressed as a Gypsy fortuneteller. Jack was a doctor, disguised in a surgi-cal gown and gloves and mask Sheridan brought home from the hospital. Tōsi was a pirate and Lily was a ghost in a sheet. Anna surprised them all. She was dressed as an island girl in a holoku, with her hair loose down her back and pinned with flowers. She used make-up to darken her face and hands. When Lily first saw her, at the end of the hall, she thought it was Christmas come back, but she heard Anna laugh and her heart began to beat again.

All assembled, excited and giggly, a little frightened to be going out in the dark with only a lantern, they left the Big House, children and mother, and went down the dusty cane road to their closest neighbor, one mile away. Jack pulled Jessie in a red wagon. Tōsi walked behind Anna, holding her train. Lily shone in the dark, in her bed sheet. She could not see out of the small eyeholes very well, only straight ahead. Once, she turned around to look back at the house. The long line of jack-o'-lanterns they had spent the last week carving were lined up on the verandah railing, glowing gold, not that any other children would be stopping to trick or treat. They were the only children around and they were walking through the cane to the house of the plantation mana-ger and his wife.

The cane was high over their heads. Jack swung his lantern and the light swirled in and out of the tall, bowed shoots of green cane. They talked quietly. The wagon bounced and rattled and Jessie laughed very loud. Anna took her turn holding the lantern. "I hope they don't give fruit," Jessie yelled into the dark. "I won't take any," Jack yelled back. Anna always had baskets of chocolate bars waiting on the verandah. They ate the chocolate through the year until the next Hallowe'en.

The plantation manager, Mr. Danny, and his wife were waiting for them. The children's high voices hummed across the fields and warned them they were coming. The light from the lantern lit up the cane from below, not in a single beam of light, but in a diffused yellow circle that moved jerkily along. The Dannys were waiting for them on their front porch, silhouetted by the light from inside. Mrs. Danny wore an apron over her muu-muu. They were as excited as the children and pretended to be frightened by the strangers emerging from the field, faces hidden in masks and sheets, or perhaps the visitors really were frightening, bare and dusty brown feet the only sign that they were not apparitions.

They did not recognize Anna. She was very excited. Lily could feel her body buzz with nerves as they brushed against each other and squeezed through the narrow doorway into the front room. Mr. Danny lifted Jessie out of the wagon and carried her into the house.

It was very bright inside but still they did not recognize Anna. Mrs. Danny made each of them step forward and tried to guess their disguises and their names. "Oh, a surgeon!" she said to Jack. He nodded his head. She held out a big bag of rock candy.

Lily watched her mother. She was at the back. She sidled over to the dining room table and, without trying to hide it, began dropping Mrs. Danny's old heirloom silver into her trick or treat sack. They did not notice at first, but then Mr. Danny heard the noise as a sugar bowl clanged against a spoon at the bottom of the sack and he nudged his wife, who looked up just in time to see her favorite cake cutter disappear. Jack and Jessie were busy filling their own bags, but Tōsi and Lily watched Anna with delight. When Anna saw the Dannys staring at her, astonished, she quickly drew away from the table and held the heavy, clanging sack behind her. "Who is that?" Mr. Danny asked. Anna shook her head. "Who *is* that?" he asked again, louder. She shook her head and shrugged and the silver shifted and scraped in the sack. Something about her did not invite more than inquiry. Tōsi began to giggle at Anna's prank.

Without taking his eyes off her, Mr. Danny walked to the wall telephone and called the Big House. He waited some time until Sheridan came to the line. He asked him whether he could come over right away. Nothing was wrong, he didn't think; he'd just like to see him. Yes, the children were there. When Mr. Danny looked away for one second to replace the receiver, Anna seized the moment to grab a salt shaker. Lily couldn't look at her any longer. She was afraid she would laugh. They would both begin to laugh and then the Dannys would recognize Anna's voice. Tōsi must have thought Anna was taking the joke too far, because he went to her and tried to take the bag but she held it away from him. He looked at Lily for help but she refused to give Anna away. Mrs. Danny climbed onto a chair and held her muu-muu up as if a mouse had just run across the room. Jack and Jessie finished sorting out the candy and, growing bored, looked on amiably, not understanding. Mr. Danny, eyes wide and unblinking, could not look away from Anna. He did not know what to think. "I know you," he kept saying, shaking his head.

There was the sound of a motor. Then silence and a door slamming, and Sheridan came through the open door, loose and easy, his hands in his pockets. He saw Anna and her full sack right away, but he did not betray her either. He nodded politely to Mrs. Danny and even helped himself to a few candies before he eased the children to the door, nudging them from behind, saving Anna for last so that he would not break into laughter, taking the heavy, noisy sack from her and handing it to the baffled Mr. Danny. Then he scooped up Jessie and they tumbled down the steps and into the open jeep, the children urged on from behind by him and Anna, suddenly in a rush, all jumpy and elated. No one remembered Jessie's red wagon. Once in the safety of the cane they shouted with happiness and relief.

The children, feeling the excitement, screamed and cheered, not knowing why, except that it was thrilling to be racing along the dark road, cane bending over their heads, the air cool now, and their mother and father kissing and laughing.

"You are really very naughty," Lily heard him say. The children bounced in the back. Somehow Jack lit the lantern and shone it into the field, where it leaped and careened over the cane.

"I could not face walking home," Anna said. She was sitting very close to Sheridan, over the gear shift. She kissed him. He kept looking at her and laughing. Her arm was around his neck. Lily had never felt so happy.

Anna went into Lily's room before breakfast, very cheerful and noisy. The scar down the side of her face was almost healed. She was dressed in white linen. She sat on Lily's small wooden desk. "Two things!" she said. She was very jaunty.

Lily got up slowly from bed and reached for her shorts on the back of a chair.

"Bathing suit, bathing suit," Anna said. "I am taking you and Jessie to the beach."

Lily watched her while she leafed through the school notebooks on the desk, not really looking at them, just needing something to do with her restless hands. Lily thought that she liked her better a little calmer, especially in the morning.

"I haven't woken up yet."

"I know, but this is a new day. Mornings are very important. Waking up. Starting again. Wonderful metaphors."

"Are you okay, Mama?"

"Okay? Okay?" she asked, exaggerating the word.

"I suppose I'm not used to seeing you this early or something."

"It is probably the 'or something,' but I am not going to worry about that and you must not, either. I want you to do a favor for me."

Lily exhaled. She had suspected that there was more to this visit than a swim. Always a life-or-death request when Anna wanted you to do something. Perhaps a new day for her, Lily thought, a new metaphor for her, but sweating hands for me.

"Oh?" Lily asked casually, opening her closet door and staring at the shirts, unable to choose, forgetful even of why she was standing at the closet now that Anna wanted her to do something for her.

"Yes," she said. She was almost singing. "Come here."

Lily exhaled again and went to her. Anna motioned for Lily to give her her hands. Lily held them out cautiously. Anna put two dark glass bottles into them and closed Lily's fingers around them. "There!" she said, pleased with herself.

Lily looked at the bottles. They were filled with pills. Lily looked out the window. She could see Tōsi walking barefoot across the wet lawn with baskets of flowers. He watched his feet as he walked. He looked as if he were talking to himself.

"I want you to hide them," Lily heard her say.

A milk truck creaked and swayed down the driveway. The

milk bottles tinkled gently as they rocked against each other. "So that I can never find them."

Lily turned back to her. She could see that her mother was thrilled with her act of renunciation. A new day and a new mother, smiling and reborn, sitting on her desk with her legs up. Lily felt thick and slow. It seemed as if her mother were miles ahead of her, in another solar system even, and Lily, turgid and slow to comprehend, was still four-legged and earthbound, in the swamp. Anna bounced off the desk, all crisp white and brown legs, and danced out.

Lily sat back on the bed, half-dressed, the pills still in her hands. Why doesn't she just throw them out? she thought. Just do it herself. I don't want to know about these things. I thought this sort of thing was over. She could hear her mother calling Jessie. Lily got up, all stiff and cranky, and hid the pill bottles behind some books on the shelf. She didn't feel like getting dressed. She didn't want to go swimming. She didn't want to leave her room.

She was an uncomfortable accomplice.

In the car on the way to the beach, Jessie sat in the back with Lily. Jessie had only recently agreed to be in a car that her mother was driving. Before Anna went away, one afternoon when they were coming home from a drive to the mountains, Jessie let herself out of the car at a stop sign and sat cross-legged in the tall grass by the side of the road, her arms folded across her chest, and refused to get back in the car. Anna drove on. Later, when Tōsi walked back to get her, she was still sitting there, like an Indian. So this was her first ride with Anna in some time and she was particularly attentive to road signs and yellow lights and turn signals. Anna seemed not to mind, although it must have been difficult to ignore Jessie's coughs and gasps.

They stopped at Round Head for Tigger. She and Anna had made up, although Tigger still seemed a little nervous around her, always looking sideways at her to see what she was thinking. It was impossible these days for anyone to know what Anna was thinking. Impossible even for Lily. She was most difficult to understand when she was most like other mothers. The first warning to be on your extreme guard was when she wanted to make cookies. Tigger knew this and Lily knew this, so they both watched her.

Lily could see the top half of Anna's face in the mirror. She must have known that Lily was watching her. Lily began to feel sorry for her. Everyone watched Anna and she was just trying to be normal.

"Light turning to yellow ahead," Jessie called loudly from the back. Tigger turned around to stare at her. Jessie refused to acknowledge Tigger, focused as she was on the road ahead, her eyes scanning back and forth professionally. Tigger turned back.

"I've been thinking," Tigger said, folding her hands in her lap. Anna waited. Tigger was silent. Anna turned her head for one second to smile at Tigger and encourage her, and Jessie sprang forward in alarm, but eased back when, arms outstretched and both hands on the steering wheel, Anna looked back to the road. When the car turned to the right, Jessie leaned heavily to the left. Her little foot vigorously pumped an imaginary brake. Lily forced herself to look away from the mirror. She watched instead the slip of sea glide by, blue and blurred and white.

❧

The Point behind the Big House was particularly rich in marine specimens. The porous lava rock was ideal for the formation of pools. Lily and Jack often walked out there to collect anemones and crabs and opihi. They ate the opihi raw, sucking them out of their shiny, tiny black shells. On the rocks there were several sun-bleached, white obelisks cemented there by the families of the Japanese fishermen who had been swept into the rough sea. The obelisks were covered with figure-writing, prayers for the dead, and sometimes an orange or bowl of rice was left at the base. If Lily was hungry, she sometimes ate the fruit.

At low tide, the lava spit that ran jagged and sharp into the ocean was divided into two colors by the high-water mark. Black and chalky above, pale green and leafy below. The seaweed growing below the water mark looked like lettuce. The children jumped off the Point into the ocean when the tide was high.

Lily should have been suspicious when her teacher, Mr. Mott-Smith, gave her a note to take home. It was sealed. He had written on the front "By the Kindness of Lily Shields." She gave it to her mother. Anna was sitting in the back garden. Tōsi was washing her hair with a garden hose. The soap suds rested airily on top of the tight, woven grass, refusing to sink in. Anna read the note, holding it carefully at the edges, and said, "That would be lovely!" She handed the note back to Lily. Water had dripped onto the paper, and several words had run, but Lily could still read it. Mr. Mott-Smith wrote to ask whether the seventh-grade class could come to the Point on a marine biology field trip.

Soapy water ran down the back of Anna's chair. "The limpet," she said without lifting her head or opening her eyes, "is quite an extraordinary animal. Twice a day, when the tide changes, it crawls over the lava, sucking in and filtering the sea for plankton, scratching back over the rock to its original spot. You have seen it do this many times. No one ever understood how it found its way back. One scientist with a particularly sadistic imagination filed down the grooves on its shell, suspecting that it found its way by fitting into an impression made earlier in the rock. He was right. The limpet, unable to find its place, threw itself into the ocean."

"Mama."

She laughed. "I am afraid that it is true."

Lily wished she had read the note first. She would never have given it to her.

"Don't you worry, my old sweetheart. It will be a lovely excursion, I promise." Tōsi giggled, his hands tangled in her hair. "What's so funny?" She reached behind to tickle his bare stomach, but he jumped out of the way. "What's so funny, Bugs Bunny!"

Lily turned away unnoticed and walked back to the house, listless and worried, wondering whether there was some way she could keep all those people from coming to the Big House. In her heart she knew it would be impossible to stop the expedition now that Anna had the idea in her mind.

Lily waited all that week for the note she would carry back to Mr. Mott-Smith. When Anna did not give her one, day after day, little by little, Lily allowed herself to relax. She hoped Anna had forgotten about it. It would be all right. Then one evening when Anna was on her way out with Sheridan, all bright-eyed and smelling spicy and sharp like the inside of a lacquer box, she stopped by Lily's room to say that she was looking forward to the field trip the next day.

Through the night, lying on top of the covers, Lily listened to the nightman walk around the house, heard the big car come back up the driveway, doors slamming, her father's voice, her mother laughing low in her throat. Near morning someone was up with a bad dream and walked to the kitchen. There was the brief, high scream of a kettle brought to boil, cut off suddenly with a dying moan. Lily tried not to worry. The sky lightened and the mynahs began down the lane in the banyan and she got up and dressed slowly to go to school in town, only to turn around and come back. Anna would have the whole morning to prepare for the seventh grade.

When they arrived at the house in the old blue school bus, there was no one around. It was quiet and still. There were sixteen children, including Lily. Mr. Mott-Smith asked whether she would lead, since she knew the way, so, loaded with nets and specimen cases and glass-bottomed buckets, they started across the lawn to the path. Lily looked back a few times at the house. The sky was very blue. Someone in white was shaking out a cloth on the back porch.

The path skirted the kiawe forest and ended on a bluff overlooking the Point. The morning ocean was calm. In a high wind, the rock pools disappeared, covered with milky sea foam, but the wind was low and it was still and bright. The waves swirled up and through the lava holes, and Mr. Mott-Smith shouted to them to stay away from the edge. The Point seemed to jut halfway to the horizon. Standing at the edge, it was impossible to see the bottom of the ocean. It looked miles deep where the land suddenly fell away. Some of the children were frightened.

They collected hermit crabs and big starfish and pale, transparent shrimp. Lily kept looking back at the bluff, expecting to see someone, dreading to see someone, but they were undisturbed. The sound of the waves against the rocks was very loud. They had to shout to each other.

As the sun rose higher, the sky and the sea grew brighter. It was never hot at the Point because of the strong trade winds blowing in from the Channel, but the glare hurt their eyes. Lily squinted as she looked back at the path again. Mr. Mott-Smith signaled that it was time to go, and with relief the children began to collect their equipment.

Lily suddenly did not want to go back. She had to stop them or delay them. If she jumped into the ocean she might stop them. She had done it hundreds of times but they didn't know that and it might distract them. But she saw that they had already started up the path, eager to find shade, feverish from the glare. They knew the path now and did not wait for her.

She was the last in line. They wound through the brush, past the kiawe forest. It was hot because the wind could not penetrate the thickness of sea grape and hau. Not until they reached the croquet lawn would they be soothed again by the wind from the ocean. (The house had been built especially to catch those breezes. Sometimes when all the shutters were back, the trade wind went straight through the house.)

The children dragged on through the still air, sea water slopping in buckets, pails changing from hand to hand as sea slugs expired from dehydration and crabs scuttled and scratched up the sides of jars.

Lily could see that they were almost at the end of the path. It was cooler already. Suddenly someone ahead shouted, and then someone let out a whoop, and they were running. Lily stopped. It was still possible to turn back. She hadn't seen anything. She was not yet implicated. The view to the lawn was blocked by bobbing heads. There was still time for Lily to jump off the Point into the bottomless ocean.

"Hurry up!" someone shouted and they were gone. The path was deserted. Lily could hear them at the house. They were talking. It was too late. She went ahead, hot and dry-mouthed, the water from her bucket splashing out into the dirt. The water felt cool on her feet and turned the dust into mud, which stuck between her toes.

She came out onto the lawn. Between two coral trees was a long table covered with white damask. There were pitchers of pineapple juice and lilikoi juice and silver baskets of guavas and mangoes and California plums. There were trays of little sandwiches and still-warm chocolate-chip cookies. Old Hawaiian quilts had been spread in the shade of the big poincianas. Red flowers from the trees had already dropped onto the red quilts. Tōsi gathered the marine specimens from the children and arranged them carefully under the verandah, where they would be cool and protected. The exhausted children fell onto the quilts and drank juice.

Her mother stood with Mr. Mott-Smith near the table. She was making him laugh, and he shook his head back and forth. She saw Lily and waved slightly, careful not to embarrass her in front of her school friends. She looked like a queen. She held a lauhala hat in both hands. Lily went to her.

"Hello, my little limpet," Anna said.

Lily wanted to put her head against Anna's chest and bend herself around her, fitting herself into Anna's niches, but she just nodded and smiled, as though it were like this all the time.

⌒≫

Once a week, at night, Lily's father took her to the local high school to see National Geographic travelogues. Anna was invited too, but knowing how thrilling it was for Lily to be out alone with her father, she made excuses not to go. Lily never knew that her mother arranged for them to go alone. She thought Anna was not interested.

Lily sat next to her father in the front seat of his car. She even wore shoes for the special occasion and she trembled with pleasure. She kept her hands folded, ladylike, in her lap.

The program always began, when the lights went out, with a narrator who said, "We take you back in time, to a place as yet untouched by the modern world . . ." One particular program that electrified Lily was a tour of "Olde Denmark." The song about wonderful, wonderful Copenhagen ran through her head for days. The evenings at the travelogues filled her with restlessness.

She wondered whether her father was having a good time. She worried that he would be bored and stop taking her one night a week up a brown equatorial river or through the bazaars of Tangier.

During the intermission, he would stretch as he stepped lankily into the aisle and wait for her to come out, and then they would go up the aisle together to the soda machine. People looked at them. He always asked what kind of soda she wanted, although she always answered the same, root beer. They took the frosted bottles out into the courtyard of Franklin Roosevelt High School and stood in the cool, dark night and drank the sodas. Lily had a cardigan buttoned around her neck and sometimes she was chilly but she never took it off to put her arms inside because she was superstitious about altering anything, even a sweater. Other people wandered out into the courtyard, men with bow ties and spectator shoes, schoolteachers, but they were usually alone. Lily looked at the stars through the trees.

"You're not cold?" he asked.

"Oh, no, thank you."

"We can put up the top on the way home."

"Oh, no, it's perfect the way it is. I like to see things." They stood there. He finished his soda and looked for a place to put the bottle.

"Have you been to Egypt?" she asked.

"No, not yet."

"I'd like to go."

"You'd like to go everywhere, I think."

"Yes, I would," she said.

She made him laugh and that was very pleasing. The lights blinked off and on to show that the intermission was over and they walked back inside, not hurrying, taking their time. He held the door for her and took her bottle to put in the rack next to his. He followed her back down the aisle and picked up her program from the floor under her seat. When he sat down, his long legs, crossed at the ankle, stretched into the aisle. He cleaned his eyeglasses with a polka-dot handkerchief and put them back on. He looked at Lily and smiled. She did not know then that these were her first dates and neither of them knew that only a few years later she would be gone forever.

⊂⇒🗲

As a mark of Lily's trustworthiness, Anna allowed her to take Jessie and Jack on the bus to Kuhio Beach. Their father would pick them up by the sea wall at five. It was a forty-five-minute ride and Jessie and Jack were both worried and excited. They held on to Lily's hands. They each sat in a seat by the window, watching the mountains, and Lily alternated between the two of them. They carried their bathing suits rolled up tightly in towels. Jessie kept unrolling her towel to make sure that her suit had not fallen out.

The bus stopped by the park, on one of the little streets that ran between the beach and the canal. The children got off. It was very hot. As they walked, they could hear the sound of breakers at the end of the street.

Jessie and Jack skipped ahead of her. There were no sidewalks. On the stiff lawns in front of the tiny bungalows the grass was turning brown in the heat. There were dried-out plants at the end of each lawn, fringing the houses, torch ginger and bird-of-paradise, stiff crimson and gold flowers that were not as sweet or as soft as the air Lily felt all around her. The stalks of the flowers stood out against the low, wooden eaves.

Suddenly Jack ran back toward Lily. He was pointing. Lily looked. Jessie was several houses away, frozen in place. Jack reached Lily, out of breath, and pointed again. Parked at the side of the road was their father's car.

Lily did not at first think it was strange to see her father's car there. She thought that someone at the Big House must have borrowed it. She did not, for several minutes at least, allow herself to remember what Tigger had said that afternoon at the hotel, when Anna suddenly got up and left. It wasn't until she was peering in the car window that she felt the pulse in her neck begin to beat harder and she remembered. She looked for Jack and Jessie. It was too late. They were already across the scorched lawn, in the bushes at the side of a house, their faces pressed against a window screen, shielding their eyes from the light with their hands.

She looked around. There was no one else on the little street. She thought for a minute about getting into her father's car and driving off, all by herself, but she did not know how to drive. She walked casually to the bungalow, her hands in her pockets, as if she meant to be there.

Jessie made room for her at the screen. There was the smell of perfume and fried fat. It was dark inside the bungalow, but the radio was on loud, tuned to the navy base, playing "Davy Crockett, King of the Wild Frontier." There was no one in the front room. Then the radio was turned down and they heard their father's whistle before they saw him. He came into the room with a book. He did not notice the three small, dark heads at the screen. He sat down.

It never occurred to the children that he might see them. Jessie, at one point, said loudly to no one in particular, "How did she get that stupid name anyway?" Perhaps the radio drowned them out. Perhaps they were disguised by the stems of desiccated ginger and the jade vines. They stood there perspiring, standing on scentless flowers, hands and heads resting heavily against sagging, rusted screens.

Christmas appeared in an arched doorway. She wore white ankle socks, but no shoes. She held a green parakeet on one finger. There was sweat on her forehead. She was very pretty. Lily thought her breasts were pretty. She walked across the room with her hips moving from side to side and emptied an ashtray into a straw wastebasket. The ash smoke rose as the ashes sifted through the slats in the straw onto the carpet. She turned on a dim overhead light. The bird flew away. Christmas was naked.

"The color of staph mold," Sheridan said, watching the little bird. It lighted on the sofa. Lily noticed a photograph of her father on the wall. It had once been a picture of her parents at the sailing of an ocean liner, but her mother's image had been cut off. The cut side was rough and crooked. Lily wondered whether the scissors had been blunt and whether Christmas had eaten the half with her mother on it.

Christmas sat down with a plop in a wicker rocker and turned the radio a little louder. The song was "Blueberry Hill." Lily could hear Jack quietly singing to himself.

Sheridan looked around for an ashtray, and Christmas got up quickly to get him one. He smiled at her. Her arms were dimpled and brown. They were no longer bruised.

"I'll make you some Kool-Aid or something." She walked out of the room and Sheridan put his book down and followed her. Lily could not see them, although the kitchen door was open and she could hear Christmas laughing. Lily could not hear her father, only a scratching noise. She looked down, squinting from the light, and saw Jack picking a small hole in the screen, putting his finger in the hole to make it larger.

"Stop leaning on me!" she said to Jessie. Jessie's eyes filled with tears. "Well, don't," Lily said furiously. Jessie confused her by crying. Jessie never cried. She wiped away the tears and stepped away from Lily sadly. Lily wanted to push her and she wanted to comfort her. But she just stood there. Everything seemed to move in slow motion, as though she were underwater, paddling with thick, exaggerated strokes. The water oozed between her fingers.

Then Jack began to cry. Jessie jumped back from the screen and crouched under a bush. Lily knew she must stop Jack from screaming. It took a long time for her to swim to him. She had to lift her legs high and really pull with the breast stroke.

She saw movement out of the corner of her eye. She turned slowly to the side, careful not to displace any water on her brother and sister — it might frighten them — and she saw that the kitchen door had just closed. It swung back and forth in short, quick jerks, then stopped.

∽✜

Sheridan pulled up in front of the sea wall at five o'clock. They were sitting on the wall holding the rolled-up towels with the dry bathing suits inside, waiting for him. He did not notice that they were oddly subdued or even that their hair was not wet. They had not been in the water.

Jack sat in the front. He stuck his head out the window. The wind blew his thin brown hair straight up off his scalp and he looked like a crested bird. Jessie was holding hands with

Lily in the back. Sheridan cheerfully asked Jack questions about school and Jack nervously popped his head in and out of the car with each answer. Lily thought it would get on her father's nerves, but he was relaxed and gay. He was not like that often.

It is because of her, Lily thought. My mother does not make him lighthearted, I do not make him lighthearted, Christmas does. It was then that Lily decided there was no hope. She understood how he felt. Christmas was simple and pliant. Anna was unpredictable and complicated. She made you nervous and upset. Christmas was just glad to see you. She probably never thought of love, except as Valentines, and music you could dance to. Anna took advantage of you if you loved her.

Once, when Lily was carrying Anna down the hall she asked Jessie why she would not help her, and Jessie stood stubbornly at the end of the hall and said, "She drives a car, it goes through a wall; she cooks, the kitchen catches on fire; she swims, she gets caught in the undertow." Jessie, although she was seven years old, thought like Sheridan. Their patience had run out, and their willingness to be surprised. But Jessie also bit her nails down past the cuticle until her fingertips were red and swollen and when there was nothing left, she started on her toenails.

Jack was a sleepwalker. He just observed. He did not ask questions. He talked to his pigeons. Sometimes he got up in the middle of the night and sneaked out of the house to the pigeon coop. Lily followed him once because she was worried. He sat in the grass in front of the cage and talked to the birds about his mother. After that first time, although she heard him leave the house many times, she did not go after him, but watched from the gallery until he returned.

And here we all are, Lily said to herself, riding along in the station wagon, back from Kuhio Beach, with Father chatting merrily to Jack about the difference between growing sugar and Virginia tobacco, and Jessie and I in the back, all witnesses, headed for home and Mother. She was terrified that Jack or Jessie, in their nervousness, would tell her right away: he has been to see Christmas. She made Kool-Aid and picked up newspapers from the sofa. He spent the afternoon there.

Lily knew she would not tell anyone, not even Tōsi. But what if Anna knew without anyone having to say so? Perhaps they looked different. What if they started giggling or what if there was evidence, dried plumeria stuck in their hair, screen marks on their foreheads, or worse yet, what if she could smell Christmas on them? She probably will smell her on us, thought Lily.

Lily felt sick to her stomach, like stage fright. She looked at Jessie and Jack but there was nothing that showed outwardly. She examined herself. She ran her tongue over her teeth. She smoothed down her hair with her perspiring hands. She cleaned the sand from under her short nails, then stopped suddenly, thinking she should keep the sand under her nails; she might need it as proof that they were at the beach, not anyplace else.

Sheridan turned in to the driveway. Jack and Jessie looked at Lily. She shook her head, trying to warn them without saying it, not knowing what to say, and the car stopped at the front and they got out, talking and gesturing all of a sudden.

She was waiting for them at the top of the steps, on the verandah, happy to see them, pretty and calm, not goofy, regretting that she had not gone with them now that they were back and she could see what a good time they must have had. She embraced them. She did not smell anything. She held Lily's chin in her hand and looked at her, but not any harder than she always looked at Lily, which was quite hard, since she always worried about Lily and tried to guess what she was thinking. Lily forced herself to look into her eyes. Anna smiled and let her go. She knows, Lily thought. She doesn't know.

Jack and Jessie noisily squeezed past her. She did not notice their nervousness. She waited in the doorway for Sheridan while he came last up the steps, holding a stalk of red torch ginger behind his back. She kissed him on the lips and he handed her the flower and she said something nice and he followed her inside, laughing.

TEN

*W*HEN I TELEPHONED JESSIE from the Miami airport
to tell her where I was going, she said, "You sure like
islands."

"I like the sudden changes in the weather."

"You don't think it has to do with the mother's body? All
that water, surrounded by water? Coves. What about coves?"

She made me laugh. I told her that she wouldn't have to
worry about her Bank of Maui card anymore. Sheridan had
made her rich. The bill that I paid to the lawyer was for a
codicil they had drawn up for him, dividing his estate in exactly six months' time. That meant, too, that his disappearance, if I could keep calling it that, was not an accident. He
had arranged with the lawyers that I receive the envelope in
the same six months.

I was surprised that Jessie did not have much interest in
him. "Well, he's not here," she said breezily. "No one's seen
him."

Even Jack had not sounded concerned in his letter. He was going to Harvard. He was going into politics, he wrote.

They were both, however, very excited about Tōsi. Jack had noted in a P.S. that the American pilots carrying the atom bomb had nicknamed it "Little Boy." When I told Jessie she said it was another example of Jack's idea of irony.

"You're not looking for Father," she said as I was about to hang up.

"I don't know," I said. She made me so nervous. I felt angry, too, that she should be able to make me feel embarrassed about looking for our father.

She was incredulous. "Whatever for?"

To my surprise, I found I could not repudiate him. "Perhaps he's in trouble," I said meekly.

"Not him. He's way past trouble."

I didn't want to argue with her. "You're single-minded like him," she said after a long pause.

"Why is everyone always telling me how much I'm like him? Or her? I'm going to scream the next time someone says that."

"It's the mystery," she said calmly. "No one understands them, how they could be the way they are, so we all keep looking for clues."

I didn't answer. "You're *really* looking for clues," she said.

"I'm tired," I said and we hung up. I had a little time before my next plane left, so I went to the magazine shop and bought T-shirts for Anna and Tōsi. I watched the other travelers. They bought a lot of candy. I thought that no one looked very well. Even the children looked unhealthy and everyone seemed to be wearing pajamas. It is because I am angry at Jessie, I thought. I paid for my things.

I went back to the phone booth. In my address book, I found Ludovico Anchinelli's number. I hadn't spoken to him in two years. He was divorced and living in Asolo. He had an association with an English archaeologist, a woman in her eighties. He was interested in the past, too.

I hadn't planned to telephone him or see him, but I must have been thinking about him (the time he put the aluminum-foil tiara on the yachtsman's salad plate) or I wouldn't have been standing half-in, half-out of the booth with my book open to the A's and a handful of quarters.

It was hard to get the call through to Italy. I was impatient and irritable. Finally, the call was completed. A young-sounding woman answered the phone. He was not at home. I left word where I would be. It was hot and airless in the booth, but I was shouting my name and did not want to open the door.

"An old friend," I yelled.

"*Si, si,*" she said.

"*Si, si,*" I said and hung up. My venture back into the world was not beginning well.

My good spirits have returned. I find it surprisingly exhilarating to be traveling alone. I am not even upset about Jessie anymore. She was right: I do seem to move from island to island. I even left Venice yesterday to have lunch on another island.

I went with Tigger. I have not seen her in ten years. She lives here on the top floor of a nineteenth-century palazzo, late by Venetian standards but perfect for a Texan whose idea of the sublime is a velvet bell-pull. I have come to talk to her. I want to know about Anna and Sheridan: perhaps she will be the one to explain the mystery.

When I arrived, my little rooms were full of flowers. Ludovico had sent them. He was so happy that I had called. He is driving down to see me. I feel lightheaded and unencumbered.

In the morning when the concierge told me that the Contessa Babcock had come by while I was out, he made a funny, rolling expression with his eyes. I must have made a funny face back because he said, "Ah, madam knows," with dignified satisfaction. I didn't know. Only later did I learn that Tigger was well known "in these parts," as she would say, for drowning her late husband, with the help of her chauffeur, in the shallow canal behind the Palazzo Querini-Stampalia. The idea of a chauffeur in a city where there are no cars made me a little suspicious, in Tigger's favor, but it did not seem a completely unlikely story.

She has her pretty motorboat, which she pilots across the lagoon, wearing a well-cut sailor's suit. She has let her red hair go to gray, and she wears it short and off her face, so that when she is at the wheel, the wind blowing in from the Adriatic, she looks like a fierce hawk, eyes squinted as she makes for Torcello. Everyone knows her and she is treated with great deference, whether because she is a rich American widow or a successful murderess, I do not know.

She was waiting for me in the tiny walled garden behind the palazzo, wearing a caftan that had been dyed lavender to match the wisteria that hung all around her like little bells. The idea of a garden in Venice has always seemed to me so luxurious. Where land, solid earth, is so valuable, to give it up to pale green vines and white roses is both extravagant and surprising in a city built by shrewd and practical merchants. The garden was protected by high, damp walls. There was the slapping sound of water when a boat passed too near the outside wall.

"There you are," she said imperiously when I bent through the low door, as though she were greeting her lady-in-waiting.

"I thought we would have a little aperitivo here." I looked at my watch nervously, but I was early. I sat down on a marble bench. I could feel the dead-cold of the old stone through my skirt.

"Where were you this morning? I came by."

"Walking. Ordering dresses at Maricla for Anna." I realized that I had never liked Tigger when she was not herself. She handed me a drink.

"You know, they used to warn me that champagne made your tits sag, but it never happened to me." I began to relax. She was becoming herself. "I'm glad I didn't listen to them."

"You look very well, Tigger."

"I should hope to Christ I do. I always wore a brassiere, always. Your mother never wore one, even then, but Jesus, I'd hold them up if I went to the toilet at night." She held her breasts up through the lavender silk.

"I wanted to talk to you about her."

"I supposed you would, sugar." She drank her champagne. The fragile wisteria trembled around her when she moved. "What do you want to know, honey? God, if you're not like her!"

I decided not to scream. Maybe I was enough like Anna to make people remember her. It didn't mean that I was the same inside.

"You think I am?"

"You must be kidding! Just look at yourself in the mirror, why don't you? The same everything. When I saw you yesterday, standing there, I thought for a minute it was her, and I got chills all over my goddamn body. See, feel, even now I get them, just talking about it." She grabbed my hand and put it on her forearm, under her sleeve.

"I'm like both of them," I said. She laughed and released my hand.

"She sure was bats about him. Bats." She shook her head, still envious after all this time.

"He's gone away," I said. I could not say "disappeared" anymore. "We don't know where he is."

She shrugged. She, too, was without concern. I must have looked hurt, because she leaned forward and took my chin in her hand as if I were a child and said, "He was never really there, sugar."

I pulled myself away. "We're looking for him. Tōsi has written letters."

"I heard you two were together!" She slapped her knee. "Someone, somewhere, said they'd seen you, or a picture of you, with a little slant, your butler —"

"He has been with me since Anna was born. As my friend." I felt myself blush with temper. She lifted her eyebrows. "Not as that kind of friend, Tigger. As my real friend." My face was hot.

"Oh, I'm sorry," she said. She was amused but she had not wanted to offend me. "I mean sorry I said anything, not sorry he's not another kind of friend. I'm not one to feel any kind of prejudice in this area. You remember the boat captain? Earl Ahanu? He was a very attractive man. The strangest sensation, having those big, brown, calloused hands on you. So calloused it didn't feel like skin anymore."

"Earl Ahanu!" I shook my head and giggled like a schoolgirl.

"You're really taking me back, sugar."

"There is so much I never knew. Did you know about Tōsi?"

"You mean, how he was born?" she asked warily. I nodded. "Yes," she said. "Your mother told me. She was never good at keeping secrets."

"I wish she had told me."

She shrugged. "What would it have mattered?"

"It wouldn't have. I don't know," I said quietly. I suddenly missed him and little Anna. She poured more champagne into my glass and it foamed over onto the brick path.

"Who's this Italian beau?"

"My old friend from New York. Not a beau."

"Christ," she said impatiently. "Why not?"

"I haven't seen him in years, Tigger."

"He didn't go down the Euphrates or the Nile or the Mississippi, wherever the hell it was, with that old lady in that paper boat, did he?"

"No."

She didn't believe me.

"He paid for it."

She nodded, as if to say she had been right.

"He's coming tonight."

She nodded again, and inclined her head in approval. I was shaping up.

"I lost track of you," she said. "You never married?"

"Once, almost, just before Anna was born."

"*Qué pasa?*"

"It was the morning of the wedding. I was sitting in the bathtub, and I realized that I couldn't do it. I had to call my friend Louise to help me out of the tub because I was so pregnant, and she was already dressed in her bridesmaid gown with a big picture hat and a basket of lilies and I splashed water on her. She was furious."

"I used to say 'Always a bride and never a bridesmaid' about myself. I like being married. I have a dependent personality," she said proudly.

"I don't think so." I realized that she was one of those women who have conservative views about marriage and children and infidelity, even though their own romantic lives

are full of sentimental license and opportunism. She dis-
approved of my being an unmarried parent. The casual
adulteries and hurried marriage ceremonies in little gray
suits, and the dazed stepchildren and half-children, and pre-
nuptial settlements, and the wintery boarding schools and
Santo Domingan divorces were all acceptable, even enviable,
if you followed the convention. The rules, like good manners,
protected you.

"I don't think you are a dependent woman," I said again.
"My mother was, but I never thought you were."

"I admired her so much. I always wanted to be like her.
She was the real thing. So refined. I used to try to be like her."

"She wasn't the real thing."

"Oh, sugar!" she said impatiently, waving me away. "If
you mean she wasn't born to it, she wasn't, I agree with you,
but take it from me, she was the real thing." She took a long
drink. "I should know."

"Do you remember the time you decided you needed
Western culture and you took me with you to see the one
Renoir at the Pacific Academy of Art?"

"Can't say that I do, sugar."

"Well, you casually remarked that Renoir painted with his
penis and I was too startled and shy to ask what you meant.
I've thought about it for years and I'm still not sure what you
meant."

She smiled demurely. "I'll show you *my* Renoirs upstairs,
sugar, and maybe you'll finally figure it out." It was the kind
of thing she might once have said to Mr. Wallenberg (not
Earl Ahanu), only then it would have been about her model-
ing pictures. She was so seductive and challenging, I could
just imagine Mr. Wallenberg knocking over his vodka martini
as he called for the check.

I laughed. "You laugh like her, too," she said.

"How did she find out about Christmas, the girl?" I blurted it out. I couldn't help myself.

She looked at me, surprised that I knew about Christmas perhaps, then shrugged and said, "Christ, she knew." She drifted off for a moment and we were quiet. "She pretended that she understood, that she was liberal-minded about these things and she would get him to confess everything, every goddamn detail, and then she'd comfort him and tell him she forgave him, but inside she was storing it all up and quietly going nuts before our eyes."

"She never went nuts, Tigger."

"No, I suppose you're right, sugar, just a little loopy, but Christ, she should have asked me. I'd have told her anything she wanted to know. I'd have helped her out."

"My grandmother says I told her."

"Maybe you did. I wouldn't give you odds. Hell, what does it matter? It's a false issue. It always was. If it wasn't that girl, it would have been something else. She loved you. All of you children. She wouldn't leave because of the children, she used to say, although I was always a little suspicious of that one. She didn't leave because she was crazy in love with him. We had a lot of fun, sugar. He was a very attractive man." She smiled. "They were a very attractive couple. The Duke and Duchess, I used to call them."

"You were a real countess once," I said, teasing her.

She snorted with laughter. "Can you imagine!" she yelled, slapping her thigh. She must have been like this when she was a girl in Texas, I thought, riding a horse, whipping him to a gallop. I was sorry she had stopped coloring her hair red.

"Now they come to me for money to restore buildings and put on operas and reconstruct the Queen of Naples' bedroom, hundreds of artistic little nancy boys running around trying to get my money. There were two of them in the apartment yesterday. Want me to finance *Ariadne auf Naxos*!" She was laughing so hard, the champagne spilled on her lavender robe, but she didn't notice.

"I remember when you went to see *Macbeth*."

"What?" She couldn't hear over her own laughter.

"I remember the old days."

"Oh, sugar," she said, standing up, the wisteria jangling in shock all around her, "how could you forget?"

I followed her down the leaf-covered path and into the palazzo. We were at water level in the cold anteroom once used as a warehouse. We started up the white marble staircase to the apartment at the top, which the count, her second husband, had left to her. The count, she told me, was killed in a freak accident in South Africa. She had been very fond of him and still kept his photograph, in a silver frame bearing his coat of arms, next to her bed.

I began to pant a little as we climbed, but Tigger was not tired. She waited patiently when I stopped to get my breath.

"You know, she said something to me the last time I saw her and I've thought of it often over the years and wondered, goddamn, what exactly she meant. I was always slow to get her drift, you know." I smiled, leaning against the balustrade.

"What was it?" I asked, afraid that Tigger would wander off and forget what my mother had said the last time she saw her. Every remark, every thought, every gesture remembered was important.

"She said," Tigger began as we started to climb again, "she said that she had done it all wrong. All her life she had believed the story about the three pigs, that if you built your house out of twigs or straw, the wolf would get you. You were supposed to be conscientious and hard-working and build your house out of bricks, while the other pigs laughed and danced, and she had done that, built a brick house. But lately she had realized what a terrible mistake she had made."

We stopped at the landing. We were almost there. "You all right, sugar?" she asked, peering at me in the dark. I nodded. She couldn't quite see me, so I cleared my throat, too loudly, and said, "Yes." The stairway grew narrower. It was no longer marble, but wood. Someone, years ago, must have tried to brighten it by covering the stairwell walls with red brocade, but it was faded, and buckled in the corners now.

"Only a few more," she said, and I followed behind her. Her back was to me and her words were lifted up inside the mildewed, vaulted stairwell and rolled back down to me.

"She had wasted her time all those years trying to build a brick house instead of singing and dancing."

"Why?" I whispered.

"Well, exactly right, sugar, that's what I wanted to know."

We had reached the top. She pushed the bell. You could not hear it ring through the thick door. We waited.

"I was someone who *had* spent her life dancing and I jealously thought all that while that Anna was doing it right, but she said no, the dancing pigs end up safe anyway."

The door opened without any warning of locks being slid or peepholes opened, as though we might have just nudged it open. A very handsome man, much younger than Tigger, perhaps my age, held the door open. He wore espadrilles and a T-shirt that said "Alcatraz." I thought he was quite an unusual butler, even for Tigger, but then she ran her hand through his greasy, black hair. Her long red nails and her enormous diamond ring were dulled with brilliantine.

"Ciao, sugar," she said to him. "Ready for a ride in the motoscafo?"

He smiled sweetly and she laughed and winked at me and shut the heavy door behind us.

⟶

I lay back on my narrow, elegant bed in the room overhanging the Grand Canal and listened to the gondoliers below talking in their odd *z*-filled dialect about a family of tourists on the other side of the canal who were waving their arms, trying to get the boatmen to ferry them across. The men spoke mockingly about the tourists, and I remembered that when we were children if a tourist stopped us on the road, leaning out red-faced from the back of a hideous, pink-striped jeep, and asked how to get to the ocean, we would give intricate instructions that in forty-five minutes would leave him stranded on the highest peak on the island.

I miss Anna. It is very difficult for me, away from her, attenuated. Childless, I become identityless. Without an Anna, I am desolate. She should not be so important. I am trying to remedy that. I am trying to improve, but I have made her my talisman: if she is happy, then I am not my mother.

Ludovico was in my little sitting room. The doors were open so that he could hear me if I wanted to talk while I waited for the operator to ring back with my call to California. I discipline myself and call Anna only every other day, before I begin dressing for dinner.

Often I dream that someone, a woman or a girl, is calling me for help and I cannot get to her. Anna, my mother, and Anna, my child. But I am much better than I used to be. Even Ludovico thinks so. He reminded me of the time he took me on a fishing trip to Vancouver Island. I had to leave two young cats behind with a friend and I insisted, frantic at the end of each day's fishing, that I call my friend to make sure the cats were all right, not dead yet. It was very difficult to find a telephone every evening. We were permitted to use the dirt logging roads only after five o'clock, when the loggers had quit for the day, so we would wait until the roads were opened and often drive miles and miles out of our way to find a telephone at a rangers' station or a gas station. Ludovico was quite understanding. I tried to control my fear. I pretended to be calm and unconcerned, but I would not be able to sleep or eat or even think until I had made the call. I kept a bag of coins in the front of the Land-Rover for the telephone. Of course, the cats were always fine.

So now, staring up at the frescoes on the ceiling, cherubs and ribboned doves after Tiepolo, I congratulated myself on being able to wait, seemingly in control, for the day's call, which would reassure me for the next forty-eight hours that my daughter was still alive.

"Hello, Tōsi? How is Anna? How are you?"

"She's fine."

"Is she there?"

"Yes, she's right here."

"Do you miss me terribly?"

Tōsi laughed, much too gaily, I thought.

"Does she?" I asked.

"We're too busy to miss anyone. We're out all day. We met some children yesterday. Very nice children."

"Oh." I was angry with him for not saying that Anna missed me and I didn't want to speak to him anymore.

"Is Anna there?"

There was fumbling on the other end. She must have dropped the telephone, but I didn't mind waiting. I was patient and relieved because I would hear her voice in a minute.

"Is she there?" Ludovico called. Cigar smoke floated out the door. She came on the line.

"Hello, Mama."

"Hello, darling."

"I love you."

"I love you."

"Me, too," Ludovico yelled.

"Ludovico says he loves you, too."

"Who is he?" She wanted to know immediately. She said something to Tōsi that I could not hear.

"He is an old, good friend of Mama's," I said.

She was silent.

"All right, darling. I'll talk to you the day after tomorrow."

" 'Bye, Mama."

" 'Bye, sweetheart." She hung up clumsily and noisily.

"Everything okay?" Ludovico called.

"Everything's fine," I said and put my hands behind my head on the pillow and noticed that the light had faded and the ceiling cherubs were barely visible, plump and round as though a string had been tied around each joint and pulled tight at wrists and ankles and elbows and knees. Anna had been a small baby.

I got up and went into the other room. Ludovico smiled at me and took some books from a chair so that I could sit down.

He is so good-natured, I thought. So even-tempered. Perhaps I had been foolish about him and not tried hard enough to keep him. It was too late, anyway. I was disappointed when I first saw him last night that I didn't fall in love with him again. I even tried to imagine him making love to me. I must have been hoping all along that I would have those kinds of feelings when I saw him again, that it would be possible for me to have a woman's life again. I suppose, now that I think about it, that is why I telephoned him in the first place. I have been thinking about love quite a bit lately. Ever since I left Tōsi and Anna I have been day-dreaming like a teen-age girl. These past few weeks, I have stupidly hoped that I was ready to live in the open, in the present. I am tired of feeling like a spy, or a ghost. Perhaps it is still too soon. I must not be discouraged.

"Don't tell me you are thinking of settling down, as they say in America." He always liked to tease me.

"Well, I am, if you must know."

"I noticed you reading all the real estate notices." He politely put out his cigar. I caught myself thinking it was something my father would have done and it made me angry at myself. "I'm surprised," he said.

"Oh, I'm trying to do the right thing. Anna must go to school soon."

He got up to push the bell for the waiter. "May I?"

I nodded. I felt distracted and uneasy.

"I used to think there were two kinds of people in the world: doctors and patients," he said.

"Uh-oh. That means you think you were the doctor."

He shrugged the way Italians are supposed to shrug, pulling his shoulders high to his ears, lifting his eyebrows and turning down the corners of his mouth.

"No one ever thinks he is the patient," I said. "Including, I might add, myself."

He laughed.

"Besides, the doctor needs the patient just as much."

"Of course," he said. "It was not meant as a criticism, Lily. I now suspect that you were the doctor all along. You seem at first as though you are not. It is really quite clever of you,

179

quite generous even. You spare the unenlightened such humiliation that way."

"Was your wife a 'patient'?"

"Lily, my dear, please. It was just a remark. A foolish one, I see. I meant to be witty. To divert you."

"Don't. Don't divert me."

"I meant to reassure you." He came to where I was sitting by the window. "You look sad, Lily. *Je suis désolé.*" He kissed my hand.

His exaggerated and ironic manner made me smile.

"I *am* sad. I realized the other day that I've been sad for a long time. But I am also fine. I am both." I jumped up and walked out onto the tiny balcony. I could hear the gondoliers going home. I wondered whether they had acquiesced and let two hundred lire overcome their disdain for the articulated tourists on the traghetto steps. Probably not, I thought. They probably left them there. I leaned over the railing. The boatmen were gone. The grape arbor was empty. They had left an empty wine bottle on a folding metal chair. I could barely see across the canal in the dusk. The tourists had gone too, given up. There was only the slap of the old, dirty water and the moon rising quickly behind Salute.

That night in Venice there was a terrible storm. I lay in bed in the dark listening to the thunder, counting the seconds between the flash of lightning and the deep rumble of the thunder. We used to do that on the plantation, caught by a sudden storm in the fields, squatting under the bamboo that swayed and bent over us: ten miles for each second you could count between light and sound.

I got up from bed, careful not to disturb Ludovico, who was sleeping peacefully. I stood at the window. With each streak of lightning, the city became even more like the after-world. I have always imagined that life after death would be like Venice — streets paved with gold, seraphim and cherubim, glittering violet and silver, and strangers speaking in a strange, sibilant tongue. I have always hoped that heaven would be like the eighteenth century.

The rain thrashed the water of the canal and sudden waves splashed up and down the steps of the palazzo, rocking the moored gondolas dangerously. With each strike of lightning, the light reflected off the huge metallic dome of the basilica and hundreds of other shining cupolas and campaniles, and off the turbulent water and back off the immense basin of clouded sky. The air smelled metallic. Perhaps that is the smell of brimstone, sulphuric, like coins in a sweating palm. The sky was electrified.

Slowly the storm began to move out over the sea. There were twenty and thirty seconds now between lightning and thunder. I slipped back into the small bed. The rain stopped. I fell asleep almost immediately.

I was awakened by my own scream. An enormous explosion of thunder, louder and more terrifying than anything I had ever heard, shook the old palace, shook the bed and the bottle of water on the nightstand. "What is it?" Ludovico asked loudly, sitting up.

"Just the storm. It sounded like a bomb."

He lay back. "Christ," he said.

"I wonder if that's what it's like." I poured myself a glass of water. The water still shook in the bottle. Perhaps it was my hand that shook. I was very thirsty.

"You screamed 'Anna,'" he said.

I didn't answer. He waited for me to speak, patient and sleepy. The rain had started again. We lay there a long time. I could tell that he was still awake because his body was not completely relaxed, nor his breathing. "If you turn on your side I can hold you," he said.

I did and he did and we fell asleep.

At dawn the telephone rang. I whispered so that I would not wake him. It was a long-distance call, jumpy with static. It was Tōsi. I could barely hear him, perhaps because of the storm.

"Say it again!" I finally had to shout.

"I've found him," I heard him say. "I know where he is."

ELEVEN

$\mathcal{T}$HE RAINY SEASON began in the spring. The rain fell
heavily and calmly, knowing it had months to go, and
because it was not cold, Lily and the children continued with
their solitary lives, only now they were wet most of the time.
Lily built reservoirs and dams in the orchard and floated
pastel barques made of shower and poinciana petals over the
falls Jessie made at the top of the hill.

The sun went down earlier at that time of year, and every
evening her father called Lily to the verandah to watch the
sun set. Often Lily left what she was doing in the fields to run
to him. Every twilight, they waited together while the sun
fell into the western Pacific. Once, she spent a week trying
to think of something to say as they stood there, and she came
up with "I like to think of it as the earth cooling off" and
when she finally said it, after practicing a little, he turned
and laughed and ruffled the top of her head. She often tried
to think of things that might amuse him, but it was not easy.

Tigger left for San Francisco for a month. Anna spent most

of the day in her room, reading. She seemed restless. She announced that she was getting a job. She bought dozens of books and sent away for pamphlets about job opportunities. She would finish a book, close it and pick up a new one from the pile next to her bed. She made lists of things she wanted to do.

Jack's bed was on her list. It was filled with stuffed animals, dogs and alligators and mice. It was so crowded that he could barely get under the covers and he would not put any of them away. She had tried removing one or two, but he always noticed and was frantic until she retrieved them from her drawers. She pretended that the animal had strolled into her bedroom only to have a chat.

She got up one afternoon, dressed, and took Jack to Osaka Dry Goods, where she ceremoniously allowed him to select a piece of cotton, white with red fleurs-de-lis, and a strip of elastic and a spool of white thread and a packet of needles, not that they did not have these things at home, and they brought them back and Tōsi carried all of the stuffed animals into her room and left them on her bed. Anna and Jack spent the rest of the day there, not letting anyone else in the room, bent over the cloth, stitching and talking in low voices, snipping here and there, sucking her finger when twice she poked it with the needle.

When they finally came out, Jack proudly carried a long, lumpy sack over his head. The roughly stitched sack was filled with all of the stuffed animals, save his few favorites. He pulled the drawstring tight and put the full sack on a shelf in the closet, where he could see it from his bed if he kept the closet door open. He was very happy and Anna was pleased. Jack could get into his bed and she could attend to the next thing on her list.

∽ঌ

Lily was late getting home from school. She had stayed behind to play with her friend, Nancy Johnson, and then she missed the second bus and had to wait. She even lingered listlessly up the road to home, stopping to rest under the banyan until she was driven on by the hundreds of noisy mynahs who gathered every evening to roost.

The house was quiet, as it usually was at that time of the day. It was a kind of limbo time, vacant and gentle, caught between ceremonies. She went straight to her room and threw her books on the bed. The light was very dim. Tōsi had forgotten to open the shutters.

She felt so dreamy that she was very startled when something in the corner moved, so slightly that she might have imagined it, an old doll falling from a shelf or a petal dropping from a flower. But then a voice said, "My old sweetheart."

"Mama?"

"Don't turn on the light."

"Are you all right?"

"Yes. Medium all right. I do not want you to see me like this. I so hoped it would be fine." Her voice caught.

"Like what, Mother? See you like what?" Lily was very alarmed.

Her mother turned on the desk light. She was huddled on top of an old toy box. Her hands were twisted and she held them together tightly between her knees. Small beads of perspiration slid down the sides of her white face into her hair.

"Do you remember those pills I asked you to hide? I entrusted them to you a few months ago."

Lily sat heavily on the bed and stared at her. She looked so pitiful and so sweet. She was frail and little. She had lost her fierceness. She always did try, Lily suddenly thought. My mother tries very hard.

"Oh, Mama," she said quietly.

"I need to take them," she said simply. She was short of breath. She managed to pull her hands from the tight grip of her bony knees and she looked straight up at Lily, her self-respect returning as she told the truth. "I never imagined it would be like this. Never. I did not ever become the woman I hoped to be. Perhaps the woman my mother wanted — I think I did accomplish that in some greedy way — but not the woman I secretly dreamed of becoming. Funny."

"What did you want to be?"

"Oh — " she said and stopped, as though the question held too much weight. She stared at Lily, thinking back. "It is not that I feel sorry for myself. Nothing has ever happened to me that I did not in some way intend. It is just that I have known so little and so poorly how to make things right."

"Everything is all right," Lily said.

"Oh, I hope so, my old sweetheart." She looked around the room. She was distracted and weary. Lily felt a breathtaking pain in her heart, as though it were being crushed or squeezed. She stood up and went to the bookshelf and reached behind the books and found the two bottles of pills and gave them to her mother. Anna shook them and put them in her pocket without looking at them. Lily realized she could tell how many pills there were by the sound.

"I will be thirty-five in three weeks. It seems so young to me. I can remember when I was eighteen." She got up from the corner and walked slowly around the room, picking up old toys and drawings and maps. Once she had let Lily keep twelve live chickens in her room for a science fair experiment. Lily had won honorable mention and everyone, knowing her hopelessness in science, had been astonished, even Anna. She picked up the little diary into which Lily had copied the Gospel of St. Mark when she used to write standing at her bureau so that she could see when her mother came out of her room.

"What an odd little thing you are," her mother said fondly. "You are not at all the way I was. I was always rather dumb." She closed the diary and picked up things at random, not really looking at them, but holding on to them. "You are more like your father in that sense."

Lily was shocked. She didn't want to be like her father. She wanted to be like Anna in every way, in every detail, in every cell and dark part.

"I don't think so," Lily said.

Anna's back was turned to her. She held a doll that looked like Queen Elizabeth. "I gave you this," she said. She turned to face Lily, still holding the big doll in a silk coronation dress in her two trembling hands, but she did not look at her, she stared at the doll, not really looking at it either, but needing someplace to focus her eyes.

"He went to see Christmas."

Lily could feel her face flushing red and hot. She could not speak. She looked away.

"You do not have to say anything," her mother said. She spoke very quietly, almost in a whisper. "You see, for a long time I really thought I *was* crazy. I worked hard at trying to convince myself, and, of course, it was not hard to do, I being quite willing to assume all kinds of blame. But I don't think I want to do that anymore. In fact, I don't think I *can*."

Lily made herself look at Anna. She began to shake. Lily loved her so much that she ached. It was a yearning in her bones and flesh. Anna was calm and reflective. There was no longer any perspiration at her temples. "Not even for you," she said.

"I love you, Mama." Her mother walked to the door.

187

"Mama," Lily said quickly. "He's never been to Christmas's," she said. "I promise."

"Oh, my old sweetheart." She ran her hand slowly down the side of Lily's face and cupped her chin in her hand. Lily closed her eyes and Anna took her in her arms and held her very tight. Lily started to cry. Anna held her for a long, long time.

"My old sweetheart." She wiped Lily's face with her hands. She was smiling. Somewhere in the house the children were being called to dinner.

"I'm not very hungry," Lily said.

"All right. That's all right," she said, and still smiling, she opened the door and went out.

❧

Lily did not come out of her room for dinner. She turned out the light, opened the shutters as wide as they could go, and lay down on top of the bed.

She listened as the house went through each slow hour. Cooking time and cocktail time and dinner time and bath time and homework time and bed time. Car doors opened and shut and refrigerator doors and oven doors and dressing table drawers opened and closed and bathroom mirrors swung to and fro.

Perhaps it was because she lay there for a long time that her body seemed especially keen, alert to every sound and smell, the smell of the garden overpowering the house smells of cooking and wax and French perfume. The day flowers seemed to expel a strong scent at nightfall, as though pushing themselves in one last showy effort before, with the heat of the day, they faded away.

As it darkened, there was the new smell of the night-blooming cereus and the jasmine. The house quieted, leaving the faint hum of appliances, radios and clocks, and an occasional stiff creak as the old wooden house stretched and sighed and cooled down.

Lily lay very still. As the room grew darker and darker, tiny flickers of light appeared and grew brighter and brighter as the dim light turned to black and the room filled with fireflies. Tiny and fluorescent, they banged and careened around the room, willfully trapped inside, crashing into walls, bumping and shining. They blinked off and on, a tiny halo of light around each. Sometimes one would venture too low and suddenly flick on its light only inches above her face. They flew very fast, back and forth, crazily, desperately, happily.

Near dawn they began to tire. One by one, their lights began to go out, as though their batteries were worn down. It was not yet the season for fireflies. They came in the summer. Lily had never seen so many inside before.

She had watched them all night. The time had gone by very slowly. Her pillow was wet on either side of her face, although she didn't know that she had cried. The last firefly burned out, arcing above her like a comet, a sparking, shooting star. It was morning.

She got up from the bed and went to the door. She opened it. Tōsi was standing there, as she thought he might be. He had come to tell her that her mother was dead.

She stood at the open window, the window where the fireflies had come in in the night, and watched as a policeman's car came up the driveway and the policeman got out, trying to muffle the sound of his car door closing as though afraid of waking someone. A white truck, not an ambulance, but a truck for transporting the already dead, arrived a few minutes later. Up until that moment the garden and house were quiet, but then slowly, like an orchestra tentatively warming up before a performance, isolated screams and sobs and moans came from all sides. There was the sound of footsteps on bare floors, heavy police feet, the bare flat slap of Tōsi's and the women's feet, someone running, the sound of squeaking wheels as a stretcher was pushed down a hall.

Then people began to appear. Mrs. Danny came quickly across the lawn, taking a short cut through the vegetable garden. She wiped her face with her apron. Ishi, the gardener, walked up from the orchard and stood in his black gum boots in front of the house. He did not come inside. There was the slam of a door, then Jack appeared, still in his pajamas, running like the wind, up the hill to the pigeon coop. The cries would stop and there would be lapses of silence before they would begin again. Lily could never tell where they would come from next.

She turned away from the window and went out, down the hall, her feet padding along now like the other sounds, to her mother's room. It was empty. She could hear people all around now, noisier and busier, telephones ringing and police radios sputtering, arrangements being made, and questions asked and answered. She could hear her father. He was talking on the telephone. He said, "I loved her so much, Mother. I loved her so much." Maybe, Lily thought calmly. Jessie was screaming in the playroom and someone was trying to soothe her but she would not stop. There were loud noises all around, but she saw no one.

On her mother's bedside table were *The Tale of Genji,* the job opportunity pamphlets, eye cream and shallow lacquer bowls of flowers, ordinary things, nothing to indicate that when she turned out the light she would never see them again. A silk robe fell over the back of a chair. On the seat of the chair was a scratched 78 record of Bertha "Chippie" Hill's "Trouble in Mind." On a Chinese table, in a silver frame, was the picture of her husband and herself at the sailing of the *Lurline,* the same one that hung on Christmas's cottage wall with her face ripped off. Everything looked peaceful and fine, as though she had intended to gaze again at the little pastels of the children, trim away the pale dead orchids from their long, quivering stems, stroke aimlessly the cool jade figurine, pick the shiny kukui-nut necklace from the drawer dusty with pink face powder, drop a pin in the clay ashtray Jack made at school, live her quiet life for years to come.

There was an indentation on the pillow where her head had rested. The top sheet was thrown back. On the bottom sheet Lily could make out the faint outline of where her arms and back and legs had lain. The creases and folds made an outline of her body. Lily touched the sheet. It was still warm. It was damp. Perhaps it had been too warm for her in here, she thought angrily. She looked around at the French doors but they were wide open.

Tentatively and very gently so as not to disturb the impression of her mother's body on the sheet, Lily sat down on the edge of the bed. She lifted first one leg, then the other, and very carefully fitted them into where her mother's legs had been. Lily's legs were not as long as her mother's, so naturally they did not fit into the indentations perfectly, certainly not down to the heel marks, but it was a rather good fit. Then Lily very slowly eased herself back, so that her head lay on the pillow and her arms lay still along her sides where her mother's had lain.

As soon as her head was on the pillow, she could smell her

mother's scent, strong and sweet, a little like ripe peaches. The pleasure of her smell was unbearable. Lily never wanted to move. She closed her eyes. She stayed there a long time, still and outstretched, in her mother's niches at last, while around her, without her, the real world recovered and resumed.

TWELVE

LITTLE ANNA AND TŌSI were very happy to see me. To my surprise, my time away from them had been pleasant. In the end, I did not feel as incomplete as I am accustomed to feeling when I am away from them. Perhaps Ludovico helped. He promised to visit us, or better, to meet me somewhere, now that I realize I can leave Anna behind and she will not die.

She whispered to me that she had cried herself to sleep every night I was away. She slept in the same room as Tōsi and she was hurt because he had told her, every night when she cried, to stop sniffling. In the past, I would have been secretly pleased that she had missed me so much. She was surprised when I did not take her side against Tōsi, but I no longer feel pride that a child has wept for me in the night. As she whispered to me I could feel the damp pillow against my own cheek: it was too much like myself and the other Anna. I no longer want Anna to need me that much. Or perhaps what I mean is that I no longer need her, need them, Anna and Anna, so much. I have had them on both ends of me for so long. My bookends.

Tōsi and Anna were staying with Anna's father. He is tall, quiet and fatherly. He has always been very nice to me, kind in that same detached and seemingly harmless way as Sheridan. I wondered as I watched him at lunch whether it wasn't the easiest way. His girl friend was there, too, and he told me so many times that she was wonderful with children that I began to think he meant me, she would be wonderful with me. They were eager and earnest and Anna seemed very happy. Tōsi was quiet, having slipped into some self-sufficient state of meditation. I noticed that he hardly even blinked. Anna and her father's friend skipped around the small garden, pretending to be butterflies.

I asked Mark whether he minded keeping Anna for another few weeks. He said he didn't mind at all and went to be a ladybug. I could feel, rather than see, Tōsi staring wide-eyed at me. While I was away, he had begun wearing only Western clothes. He wears white Korean Ping-Pong shoes instead of tabis, and linen suits. He looks very handsome. He is tall for a Japanese and very slender. He resembles my father, at least in his way of putting clothes on, dropping clothes on really, it is so casual. (Every man I see seems to remind me of my father. This is a recent habit — years have gone by when I did not think of Sheridan. Or so it has seemed. I refuse to encourage this. I want the opposite. I want to be free of him. And Anna, my mother, and the sound of the trade winds and the ever-sickening smell of gardenias and the feel of imaginary guava seeds stuck between my teeth. Perhaps that is why I am going to find him: find him in order to let him go.)

"Do you want to come?" I asked Tōsi.

"I've already packed," he said quietly. "I was going anyway."

Mark came up behind me, his pipe covered with bright yellow pollen. The girls were still hurling themselves through the bushes.

"Where are you going?" he asked. "If you don't mind my asking." He treated me carefully, as though I had an explosive nature. It made me self-conscious.

"To find my father."

"Oh?" He raised his eyebrows and made an expression that seemed to imply that he had been through all this before.

"I don't mean it metaphorically." I sounded a little snippy.

"Is he all right?" he asked apologetically.

"I don't know."

"She has a theory," Tōsi said.

"I do?"

"You know, the one about Napoleon," Tōsi said.

Mark relit his pipe patiently, snapping open and shut his old Zippo lighter. He watched me through a cloud of smoke.

I took a breath and said, "Mental hospitals are filled with people who are relatively harmless, who can take care of themselves, learn to type, make field trips to the zoo, and even have relationships with other patients. They seem quite normal except that they think they are Napoleon or Elizabeth Taylor. The only difference I ever saw between the man in the booby hatch who thinks he is Napoleon and my father is that my father thinks he is Dr. Sheridan Shields and his idea of a field trip is five weeks in Tahiti."

There was a long pause. "Very witty," Mark finally said, shaking his head. "Very witty."

"But that's not exactly the point," I said but he had gone to take a thorn from Anna's thumb.

The flight from Guam was long and slow. We were in a huge, old, rumbling DC-3 that had been used in the Second World War to convey troops. Above our heads were straps and hammocks and rings on cords. It was very loud and very comfortable. To my surprise, Tōsi accepted the freezing cold beer that the pilot passed back from the ice chest under his seat. There were no other passengers, only big cartons marked M'LADY HAIR SPRAY. I was not so naïve as to think that they really contained hair spray. (Jessie was right again. I did identify with fictional heroines. I was very excited.)

It was Tōsi who had written to the State Department and discovered that Sheridan had applied seven months ago for a visa to enter Cambodia. His stated purpose of visit was "Establishment of Medical Relief." Because of the war in Viet Nam and because he was not attached to any charitable organization or government agency, Sheridan had received assistance in getting his visa from an old friend in Washington, a scientist who had worked at Los Alamos in 1943.

"Everything is connected," I said. We settled in among the cartons. Tōsi stared out the window. There was nothing to see. We were inside a cloud. He seemed different, as I seemed different to myself. Before we left, he had read everything he could find about the war in Southeast Asia.

"The man who worked on the bomb helped get Father into Cambodia," I said. I was still amazed by this odd fact Tōsi had discovered.

"That time you went to Philadelphia and I asked Sheridan if I could stay in Japan, I used to ride the train back and forth past Mount Fuji. Waiting and hoping to hear from you. I refused to go to Hiroshima again. I was very lonely."

"I'm very sorry," I said. It was the first time I had ever heard Tōsi admit to a feeling of loneliness or sadness.

"Nothing to be sorry about. I became quite tired of snow-capped mountains, though."

He finished his beer and put the empty bottle down, but the movement of the plane made it roll back and forth crazily. He reached to put it over our heads in a narrow rack and he knocked down a small first-aid kit. It fell on me and opened and a disposable hypodermic dropped near my foot. I picked it up to examine it.

"They didn't have these in my day," I said.

He smiled. "I think they did, but Sheridan wouldn't allow plastic syringes in the house. He was a purist, you remember."

"I got to be quite good at using them, you know." I put the syringe back into the kit and snapped it shut. "On my best days, no blood."

"Lily-san."

"Not a drop. I had to make it about something, something other than her lying there covered in perspiration. I turned it into a game to see how good I could become."

"Maybe Sheridan will put you to work."

"Those National Geographic travelogues were never like this."

We did not know what to expect when we reached Phnom Penh. We had the name of a charter company that would fly us to a landing zone — "LZ" Tōsi called it with his new expertise — near the Viet Namese border. It was there, in the jungle, that Sheridan had supposedly started his clinic. That was all the information we had. We had money and I had brought the big envelope from the lawyers with Sheridan's papers and his special letter to Anna. I don't know why I took the envelope. Perhaps because of the letter. I was hoping he would let me read it. I believed there would be some answer in it, some solution to the puzzle. It was a discipline not to open it. I carried the envelope in a canvas fishing bag and I never let it out of my sight.

When we landed, the young pilot turned around to say good luck, although we had not told him why we were there. Perhaps he felt anyone flying into that part of the world needed luck. He was very handsome and I felt an unexpected surge of patriotism that made me laugh out loud at myself. He gave us the name of a good restaurant, Chez Mimi, and a cheap, fast tailor, Mr. Trouser. He was very cheerful.

It was so hot when we crept stiffly down the rickety plane stairs that it momentarily took my breath away. The airport was big and very busy. One plane landed after another, all sizes and all kinds. It was noisy. When our single bag was pulled out of the hold, one of the big cartons overturned and I noticed that it really did contain hair spray. The local boy shoving the cartons carelessly out of the plane saw me staring at them. He grinned and said in an exaggerated American accent, "It's a neutral country, babe." For some reason that seemed to make sense to Tōsi and he nodded sagely. "No inscrutability, please," I said. "It's too hot."

We stood where we were, confused and uncertain, until long after the plane was unloaded and the pilot had gone into town to Madame Claude's opium den. He had invited us to go with him, but we had refused. We had been instructed not even to enter the terminal.

Just as we were beginning to feel that we had been stupid and reckless ever to come, the charter man found us. He too was a cheerful American. He wore a short-sleeved white shirt and Polaroid sunglasses and carried a clipboard. "This it?" he shouted energetically as he picked up the small suitcase. I nodded and he nodded, impressed, conferring on us the status of professionals. This seemed unnecessary and as we followed him across the chaotic airfield, I wondered whether other women arrived with hatboxes and French poodles and make-up cases. I looked around but I was the only woman. There seemed to be hundreds of Americans. They looked corn-fed and healthy, like basketball stars just out of high school. "They are," Tōsi said. The Cambodians were taller than I expected and fierce-looking. I noticed that everyone stared at Tōsi. I suppose he was hard to identify. His new silk scarf only added to the mystery. He was enjoying himself, I could tell, and I was pleased for him. In the few days before we left and since then, it seemed he was becoming something apart from me, apart from the idea of us, our twinship. I was beginning to feel apart too, but I think it was his doing. He started it. I'm not sure I could have. He was no longer even convinced that it was a good idea to share the same suitcase.

The trip to Luong Savang took two hours. On the tiny plane we dozed and stared out the windows at the thick green jungle not too far below. I looked again at Sheridan's papers. I wanted to open the letter to my mother, but it was clearly marked "upon my death."

When we landed, we found a young man who spoke French to take us to the hospital in the town. He seemed to know the hospital we were looking for very well. I had brought a picture of Sheridan and in my excitement I showed it to him right away, hoping he would nod and say yes, and he did nod and say yes, but I realized it didn't mean anything. I would have to wait.

He put our suitcase in a wheelbarrow. He walked very fast. It was hard work to keep up. The streets were empty, except for two old women selling small vegetables in the empty market. The few buildings of the town were one or two stories high, made of gray cement-brick with grillework balconies. I wondered where the people were. Now and then I could hear the steady drone of an airplane at high altitude,

199

but I could not see it. It seemed wrong that the sound was comforting.

Tōsi kept up with the guide, who every ten yards turned back to me to shout "*Vite! Vite!*" as though he were afraid of losing me.

As I hurried along, I began to feel frightened. I realized that I had not sufficiently prepared myself for what I might find. My flippancy was a way of delaying my fears. Suppose Sheridan wasn't there. He could be dead. Suppose our information was incorrect. I made myself think about my father. This was no frivolous adventure. I was not in a novel. I realized that Tōsi had already thought hard about it. That was why he seemed so different. I was accustomed to his introversion, but Tōsi was showing his feelings. He was freeing himself. I was full of admiration.

The guide turned down a street and Tōsi waited for me at the corner until I caught up.

The hospital was at the end of the street. I understood then why I had seen no people in the town. They were all at the hospital, camped messily along an arcade, sleeping against walls, in and under beds, both the war wounded and newly delivered mothers, the dying and the nearly well. They were very quiet. The guide had disappeared, but the wheelbarrow with the now unimportant bag stood in the middle of the street. A woman squatting beside a dripping pipe pulled my pants leg as I passed. She grinned maliciously.

A young nun wearing an elaborate white-winged headdress stepped over the dead and living bodies as she motioned us inside. I noticed that Tōsi had removed his scarf. On the side of the building two old men were piling bodies onto a cart yoked to a water buffalo.

"B-52 strike last night," said a man's impatient, accented voice. He did a good imitation of the sound of the plane I had heard on the way to the hospital. The voice came from the courtyard. I stepped through the arcade and out again into the blinding sunlight. The courtyard was being used as an operating room, there being no electricity, and on all four sides, in the hot gloom of the porticoes, round faces hovering over black pajamas watched the man to whom the voice belonged cut off legs and arms, and dismiss the hopelessly wounded as fast as they were put on his table, concentrating on those who had a chance to survive. He was fast and ruthless. He was good at his job. I watched him stop up a chest wound with a piece of cellophane from a cigarette pack. He kept making the sound of a B-52 and once he looked up at me casually. Another young nun helped him. She must have just recently removed her cumbersome headdress, because her blond hair was cropped very short on her head and there was a white band of skin across her forehead. The faces on four sides watched without expression, some waiting their turn, some waiting to die. The ones in line for the doctor looked no different from the ones without hope. There seemed to be no relatives or friends. It was because everyone was hurt or dead. There was no one left to be a relative, keening at one's side.

There was the body of a middle-aged man, set apart from the others, along the north side of the courtyard. He had a small neat hole in the middle of his forehead. It looked like a hard scab. The doctor saw me staring at the dead man. "Caught him stealing my surgical instruments," he said. He patted his hip. I saw the blunt black tip of a pistol sticking out from under his belt. His filthy surgical smock covered most of the gun. I nodded. I looked around for Tōsi but I could not find him. The heat and the quiet and the unexpected smells of Mercurochrome and spoiled fruit filled the courtyard.

"I'm looking for my father," I said. He didn't seem to hear me. He wiped the sweat off his face with the back of his arm, but not before some drops had fallen into the open stomach wound of a boy lying passively on the table.

"Hope he didn't wear glasses," the doctor said cheerfully. His accent was French. He looked up at me and laughed. "The Khmer Rouge always shoot the ones with glasses first," he said and abruptly signaled to the nun to take the boy away.

I went into the street. Tōsi was there, talking to the other nun. The people kept clear of him, leaving a space around him, not knowing who or what he was. Asians are very prejudiced. Besides, it wouldn't have mattered anyway had they known he had been born on an evening full of death, like this one. He came to me. His new-found jauntiness had disappeared with the scarf.

"He was here," he said. "He went two days ago with a nurse to a village on the border where there was typhoid. These are some of the survivors here." He stopped. He wasn't sure I had understood. He pointed to the old men squatting by the curb, blank-eyed and silent. "They saw him. He was treating them when the Khmer Rouge came. The farmers hid him in a hut. Then the B-52s came."

I understood. "We must go there," I said. "He'll need us."

"When the planes came, they tried to stop him, but he ran out of the hut and the Khmer Rouge saw him. They may have survived the bombs and gone back into the forest. Taken him with them as a prisoner."

"He would have been valuable to them perhaps."

Tōsi shrugged. He was listless and nervous at the same time. He kept looking out of the corners of his eyes. I took him by the hand and led him back up the street to a deserted food stall and we stretched out on two lengths of rough boards held up by chalky cement bricks. There was a crater in the middle of the road. The old women were gone.

We stayed in the town for a week, sleeping sometimes on our boards, sometimes on a mat in the district chief's house. We hired two young army deserters, who took us by foot to the border village where Sheridan had gone to inoculate the farmers. There was nothing there. You could not say it was deserted. There was nothing but mud and dust. There was not even a flattened banana tree. One of the boys kept smiling and pointing to the sky in admiration of American technology. We camped on the edge of what once was the village, facing the jungle so that we would not be caught off guard by the rebels. It did not seem particularly adequate protection to me. The boys still had their guns and ammunition, so we slept under tents of the Cambodian army with the letters FANK stenciled on the sides. We were guarded with submachine guns from China. "Very much valuable," one ex-soldier told me, patting his gun proudly. But they were nervous and eager to get back to their families, and after bargaining for more money (dollars only), they refused to stay another night in the bomb-cleaned clearing. All week long when I had not stood staring into the jungle, I had picked and scraped in the dirt, looking for a sign, looking for belongings invulnerable to TNT, like the lucky survivor of a house fire, but there was nothing, not a shard, not a coin, not a hope.

On the way back to the hospital town, we stopped in every village, in every dark hut, in every rice paddy. We found one man who said he had seen two wounded guerrillas leading a tall, white man north into the Sanctuaries but he also said that Sihanouk was his uncle. Perhaps he was right about both. There was no way to know.

I saw the French doctor only once before we left. He was

bathing in the small irrigation ditch that ran parallel to the rice paddies. The water was shallow and muddy but he was enjoying himself, lathering happily under his cadaverous arms and between his legs.

Tōsi and I did not speak much. We were too busy, in a way. We were too preoccupied. Toward the end of our month there, the rest of the terrified townspeople began to return one by one from their caves and tunnels in the jungle and Tōsi became, for a day or two before we left, an object of veneration. It was an honor to touch him. He did nothing to encourage this; in fact, he was taciturn and even forbidding, but they named him the Man-Who-Was-Not-Anything because they could not believe that he was not Viet Namese or Chinese or Laotian.

If Tōsi and I had not been together, it would perhaps have been impossible ever to leave. I, at least, had Anna waiting for me across the world. And Tōsi had his objectivity.

"If he came here, during a war, having settled all of his affairs first, perhaps he wanted to be lost," he said. He spoke without bitterness or anguish. To him, it seemed an acceptable choice. Maybe it even seemed a desirable choice. I don't know.

"Suicide is a mortal sin," I said. I meant it ironically, but Tōsi considered it seriously for an instant and then shrugged.

"We've done everything we can," he said. "To stay any longer would be dangerous. Besides, he would be insulted."

The day we left, we both felt a last-minute panic that we should stay and continue our search. I even found it difficult to exhale and I had to stand bent over to force the air from my lungs. Then the small plane landed to take us away and it seemed too late to change our minds and Tōsi, anyway, insisted that we had done as much as we could.

We could not get onto any commercial plane out of Phnom Penh, but somehow the inexplicably good-humored American charter-plane man managed to get us onto an Air Indochina plane that stopped briefly in Saigon, then flew on to Honolulu. Tōsi had telegraphed ahead, and Jessie and Jack would be waiting for us at the airport. We would have a few hours together before Tōsi and I left for Los Angeles. I calculated, with the help of the charter man, that I would be with Anna in time for dinner the next evening.

Our plane was in line on the runway, its engines already started, when the heavy door was suddenly pulled open and a young man in army boots and civilian clothes was thrown inside. He almost landed in my lap. The seats had been taken out of the plane and Tōsi and I sat on the floor on either side, our backs against the chilly metal sides, our legs stretched into what once had been the aisle.

The man righted himself clumsily and settled in next to me, near the pilot. The pilot looked back over his shoulder through the open cockpit door and waved at the man. The man smiled and waved back. It said "Cooper" in black ink on his boots. He took a bottle of Southern Comfort and a plastic pouch of marijuana from a native straw bag. He rolled a cigarette. He was about twenty or twenty-one.

"Saigon?" he asked.

"Just stopping there," I said politely. He lit the cigarette and took a big drag and stretched lankily to pass it to the pilot, who smoked a little. Cooper waited patiently until he got it back, and passed it to me. He kneeled to look out a window as the plane left Cambodia. He stayed there until he could no longer see the ground, his forehead pressed against the rain-streaked glass. The plane flew heavily. It was a long trip.

"I'm going back to LBJ," he said simply. Tōsi nodded.

"Long Binh Jail," Tōsi said to me. Cooper sat down and I pulled my fishing bag closer to me to make room for him.

"Where you from?" Cooper asked. I wasn't really listening.

I wanted to think about my father and my mother and I had been waiting eagerly for a quiet time such as this, but now this man, this kid, was sitting next to me, hungry for conversation and attention.

"You work for the 525th, right?" he said to Tōsi, pretending to be worried. Tōsi just smiled, making it seem true. "Military intelligence," Tōsi mumbled to me.

"You don't act as if you're going back to jail," Tōsi said.

"I made the big fucking capital crime of marrying a gook," he said, smiling. I looked at Tōsi, but I realized that after the past month, he was beyond racial slurs.

"Her brother was a VC," he said. "After Ia Drang in 'sixty-five some of her family was chased into Cambodia. When I escaped from fucking LBJ" — he gave a loud cowboy whoop — "her old lady got me across the border."

"How did you get caught?" I asked. He was both repellent and irresistible.

He shrugged easily. "Fucking MPs would have wiped me if they caught me going over the hill." He smoked some more. "I was lucky," he said quietly.

The plane rumbled and rolled on its way and Tōsi fell asleep and eventually Cooper dozed off and I was left to myself in the rocking, soothing airship. I could see the red and green lights of the instrument panel and hear the pilot on the radio now and then. Earth to Mars, Earth to Mars, do you read me? I thought.

Once Cooper woke up abruptly and said disconnectedly to me, "There are three thousand fucking guys AWOL in Soul Kitchen in downtown Saigon and they go after me." He lay back and closed his eyes and said to no one, "I'm just a poor motherfucker in love." He fell asleep again.

After about an hour I could begin to think about Sheridan, and Anna, and all of us. I remembered some things about

Sheridan. Not big things, but that he could strike a match with his thumbnail and whittle; sentimental things. He would have been embarrassed by anything sentimental. I would have given anything to see him alive. I felt a tiny envy and pride that he had gone to the jungle. I wondered what had made him give up the Big House. Perhaps, after all, the exquisite had no longer been enough for him. He was a hedonist and a martyr and both require a kind of narcissism. I hoped I could keep one Buddha, the one he had unwrapped for me the morning I went to see Fan. When we get home, I thought, I will give everyone their money, their share of treasure, their gifts from Sheridan and Anna. Jessie can stop worrying. Jack can become a senator. Tōsi can go. He will have his own life. Perhaps I really will live in one place, get a job, raise cocker spaniels. I was ashamed that I felt so sad. I wanted to feel full of hope. The idea of Tōsi leaving, of Sheridan dead — as Anna once said, it was not how I had imagined it would be.

The man woke with a scream. "It's okay, Cooper," I said. "It's okay."

He leaned back and covered his eyes with his arm. "I'm not Cooper. Cooper's dead." He sat up wearily and drank from the bottle of Southern Comfort. He offered me the bottle with his mouth full of whiskey but I didn't feel like drinking. He fell back and swallowed. "These are just Cooper's boots," he said.

The jovial voice of the pilot came over the loudspeaker. "You want to pass some of that up this-a-way?"

The soldier passed the bottle good-naturedly to the cockpit. I began to think about rescuing him. Perhaps I could help him, Tōsi and I could. When we landed in Saigon, we could help him to escape. He had no handcuffs. He wasn't bound. The pilot was obviously sympathetic. We had some money.

"There's a kid in LBJ fourteen years old," he said to no one in particular. "They got him hidden in fucking solitary 'cause they're afraid some big-shot reporter from NBC might find out how young he is and blow the roof off." He rubbed his eyes. "He was a fucking volunteer!" He laughed.

The pilot passed the bottle back and said that we were landing in Saigon. Tōsi woke up, confused for a minute. He reminded me of when he was a child. The soldier put away the grass and the Southern Comfort. I could feel the plane begin its descent. I slid over to Tōsi to explain my plan for helping the soldier to escape, or rather my idea to help him escape, because I didn't have a plan yet. I just knew we should help him. Tōsi listened. He did not look at me as if I were crazy, but he did not come up with any great plan either. "Surely we could help him," I pleaded.

I hardly noticed that the plane had landed. Tōsi and I were not to leave the airfield, as the plane would refuel quickly and we would be off again, but the pilot had said that we could stretch our legs. The door swung up with a whoosh of sudden noise and heat from the outside and I turned to whisper to the soldier that we would help him.

I was shocked to see that he was gone, and that he had taken my bag with him. He had taken Sheridan's letter to Anna. I hadn't been quick enough. I had wanted to save him, and he had stolen my bag. I leaned out the door, but it was already sundown and I could only see the skeletal outline of an electrical platform, and the pilot loping bowlegged into the mist. I had wanted to help Sheridan, too. And Anna. Now they were both dead and I was sitting in the dark underbelly of an old B-29, with Tōsi struggling to stay awake next to me, perhaps the same B-29 that had flown over his mother on Koi Bridge the day the world had ended, and I would never, ever know what my father had to say to my mother upon his death.

"Tōsi." I nudged him. "Tōsi." I thought I was going to vomit.

In his sleep, he had eased down onto a pile of folded parachutes. He straightened up and stretched out his legs. His top-heavy canvas shoes toppled over and the white rubber heels squeaked against each other.

"My mouth is so dry," he said. He shivered in the new air. I had heard him say "Lily" in his sleep.

"He took the letter," I said. I started to cry.

He had been looking around for something to drink, but he turned to stare at me and it seemed as though his eyes were suddenly full of weariness; not sleepiness, but another kind of exhaustion. My compulsion had exhausted him, had exhausted us both, and it was not over yet.

"I have it," he said. "I took it for safekeeping." He pulled Sheridan's letter out of the pocket of his jacket and handed it to me.

"You should have told me," I said, wiping my eyes with the backs of my fists like a child.

He leaned his head back against a small window as I yanked the letter out of its now mud-stained and ragged envelope. It was written on a single piece of cream-colored paper, folded in half. I unfolded it and read aloud. My voice cracked.

"'My dear Anna. Since I assume that all of the really important things will have been said and felt and done before either of our deaths, this note concerns itself with more practical matters. As you know, Mr. McWalter in San Francisco is at your disposal. He understands fully all of the provisions in my will and will also undertake any investments you or the children may wish to make.'"

I looked at Tōsi. My heart was beating very fast. He nodded to me to continue. The big spotlight from Tan Son Nhut swept back and forth across the runway, and because my back was to the door, its light shone again and again on the piece of paper in my trembling hand and on Tōsi's smooth face.

" 'The only thing on which I must insist is that you resist, with McWalter's help, any efforts of the big sugar and land interests to buy the plantation.' "

I felt that I could not read fast enough to dispel my increasing disappointment. As little Anna would have said, I had not gotten to the good parts yet, and the letter, from what I could see, was not particularly long. I turned it over. Halfway down the page it was signed, "I love you, S."

"It's so like him," Tōsi said, shaking his head in resigned admiration.

There was a new smell of gasoline, as well as a smell of salt and brine. I felt giddy and lightheaded. I thought perhaps it was the combination of the gasoline vapors and the sweeping, arcing light.

I read, " 'I am sure that you will manage very well. You have tremendous strength. I have always thought that about you. You have the kind of strength that I most admire. Unlike mine, yours is without vanity or sly bravery.' "

I felt myself getting lighter and lighter. There was no mistaking the feeling. I had known it once before, the night Sheridan gave the party at the Big House and my wet hair got caught in the chandelier, the night I saw Anna standing in the corner and I could not get to her. I still cannot get to her, I thought. Only this time, it is not so frightening. I am not confused. I have a strange sense of relief.

Tōsi leaned toward me, and I saw that he was smiling as he snatched the letter from my hand.

" 'The orchids do not need any particular attention beyond what Ishi gives them,' " he read, " 'but I assume (as he is now in his sixties) that he will want to retire to Hokkaido eventually. The Orchid Show that is held in Hilo every year is often quite a good place to find . . .' " Tōsi turned the page over and read the last few lines to himself. " 'I love you, S,' " he said, and his hand, holding the letter, dropped heavily, and with finality, into his lap. He was smiling.

I had carried this precious letter with me throughout Southeast Asia for many, many weeks. Even when I slept, it had never been more than an arm's reach away, and when I did sleep, I dreamed about what it would tell me. Now I could only laugh. It *was* very like Sheridan.

I slid across the floor so that I was next to Tōsi, facing the light. It was drizzling and the puddles of water and gasoline and reflected light were like the backs of mahimahi. I leaned close to him. I realized that I had not touched him in years: his body was no longer that angular length of bones and bruises that I remembered from long ago when I used to fall on him from trees.

I imagined, as I felt him wipe the perspiration from my forehead with his cheek, that one could probably grow accustomed to viewing the world from a great distance. No one else even need be aware of the oddity and the loneliness of it. I was thrilled, when I felt his mouth on my neck and in my hair, that the tear-drop crystals caught there did not alarm him, but just as I was struggling to transform my enormous height into a virtue and a gift, and turning to find his smiling, calming face, I was elated to feel myself slowly becoming my own size again. There was no longer even the tinkling sound as the crystals disentangled themselves and disappeared, upward, into the dark.

ABOUT THE AUTHOR

SUSANNA MOORE grew up in Hawaii and lives in Europe and New York City. *My Old Sweetheart* is her first novel.